MARIE'S HOME

Also by CAROLINE AUSTIN

Dorothy's Dilemma: A Tale at the Time of Charles I
Hugh Herbert's Inheritance
Cousin Geoffrey and I
Unlucky: A Fragment of a Girl's Life

"MADEMOISELLE DE LA FONTENAYE, I PRESUME,"
HE SAID AT LENGTH   *Page 121*

Marie's Home

Or, A Glimpse of the Past

BY
CAROLINE AUSTIN

Illustrated by GORDON BROWNE

Salem Ridge Press
Emmaus, Pennsylvania

Originally published
1885
Blackie & Son, Limited

Republished 2006
Salem Ridge Press LLC
4263 Salem Drive
Emmaus, Pennsylvania 18049

www.salemridgepress.com

ISBN-10: 0-9776786-5-2
ISBN-13: 978-0-9776786-5-5

PUBLISHER'S NOTE

For us the French Revolution happened in the distant past, but when *Marie's Home* was written, less than 100 years had elapsed since the Revolution. By having a present-day girl receive her great-grandmother's journal, the author, Caroline Austin, connected momentous events of the past with the lives of her readers. This also serves as a reminder to us that history happened to real people, people that are part of our own family's story, even though they lived a long time ago.

In *Marie's Home*, Marie's father tells her, "If we would find happiness in this world we must go where duty calls, and be loyal and patient even though things seem hard." This concept of doing our duty even when it is difficult is no longer commonly held as a virtue in our society but that does not mean it is any less important for us. Marie's parents lived by these words and Marie did her best to follow in their footsteps. Throughout the story she consistently demonstrates courage, compassion, self-sacrifice and true nobility. May we all learn from her wonderful example.

Daniel Mills

August 2006

CONTENTS

ILLUSTRATIONS

MARIE'S HOME

MARIE'S HOME:
OR, A GLIMPSE OF THE PAST

CHAPTER I

FIFTEEN!

A BRILLIANT day in June, the sun shining, the morning air already laden with warm breath of roses and of new-mown hay. The sun had been up for hours though it was still early, and he was touching with golden light the curious red-tiled gables of an old house—so old that people used to come for miles round to see it, and to fancy, as they gazed on it and walked round the old-fashioned garden full of sweet-scented flowers, that they were back in the days of Good Queen Bess.

There was a terrace-walk, its stone balustrade gray with age, and leading to it were steps worn by the feet of many generations. Below there was a yew-tree walk of softest grass; the trees which bordered it were cut into most curious shapes of people and of animals; and a marble sundial, round which carved figures of the hours were dancing, stood at its further end.

The sun in his travels went peeping through a latticed window whose casement stood open, and fell upon the face of little Marie Hamilton, who opened her eyes and jumped up quickly.

"Just the right sort of day for a birthday," she said, running to the window and looking out upon the garden all ablaze with flowers, where the birds were singing their sweetest songs.

She was soon ready, and, leaving her room, she ran quietly along the corridor and down the old oak staircase. In the hall she paused. The door was open, the sunlight was pouring in, and glancing on old portraits that adorned the walls.

Marie looked round her thoughtfully, then moved on a few paces until she stood beneath the picture of a little girl in the dress of a hundred years ago. The cap was of soft muslin, the petticoat of pink satin, quilted, the body of muslin crossed in front and tied behind. Long mittens, clocked stockings, and high-heeled shoes completed the costume, which looked as if made on purpose for a fancy ball. But it was not on these that the eye of the beholder was wont to rest. The greatest charm of the picture was in its face, which, though not regularly beautiful, was strangely sweet. The mouth was smiling and happy, but in the soft dark eyes there was a tremulous wistful expression, telling of sorrow long since felt and forgotten.

There was a likeness between the two faces, that seemed in the vivid sunlight to be gazing at one another; and the resemblance increased as Marie's look grew soft and tender, and she gave a sigh as though some sad thought were troubling her little head. As she was about to turn away, her mother's hand was laid lightly on her shoulder.

"Up already, my child?" said Mrs. Hamilton. "A happy birthday to you!"

"Oh, Mother!" replied Marie, her face breaking into smiles, "who could sleep on such a morning? I was just going to the stables to see my new pony; you know Father said I was not to see him till this morning. I was crossing the hall when I caught sight of my great-grandmother, and the sunshine made her look so natural that I stopped and began to wonder how she felt on her fifteenth birthday. It is so delightful to be fifteen! I wonder if she was as happy as I am today."

Mrs. Hamilton smiled. "Be as good as she was, my Marie, and you are certain to be happy, and to make others happy too. Here," she went on, "is my present—it fits in with your thoughts; so just look at it, and tell me what you think of it before you go."

So saying she placed a large book in Marie's hand. It was pretty to look at, for the outer cover was of velvet, on which Mrs. Hamilton had worked her little girl's monogram in gold thread; but below the velvet cover there was a curious old binding and a much-worn clasp. Marie opened it, and found that the pages, which were yellow with age, were covered with writing, still distinct, though a little dimmed by time. On the first leaf was written, "Marie de Grandville Hamilton," and beneath, "My dear Father gave me this book on my fifteenth birthday, the 4th day of January, the Year of our Lord 1793." Marie, much perplexed, looked at her mother, who smiled and said:

"This is a journal kept by your great-grandmother during the year 1793. Your grandfather gave it to me when I was married; and, knowing how fond you are of hearing our old family stories, I thought you could not have a present you would like better than this on your fifteenth birthday."

Marie's eyes sparkled. "It is the most delightful thing I could have had. A thousand thanks, dearest Mother!"

"Well, child, be off now and see your pony. After breakfast you can, if you like, spend the morning with your book in the Yew-tree Walk; that will keep you fresh for your hay-making party this evening."

The pony standing in his comfortable stall was found to be the very picture of perfection—the loveliest little beauty in the world, as he turned his soft eyes on his new mistress, and bent his neck to her caressing hand. Marie was in raptures; everything was too delightful, she said.

It seemed dreadful to waste time over breakfast on such a morning and on such a day; so after hugging and thanking her father, and swallowing a glass of milk to please her mother, she stole away with her treasure to the Yew-tree Walk, where she had dreamt more than one dream of her great-grandmother.

We will look over her shoulder and read with her a story of the past, written "long time ago."

CHAPTER II

THE JOURNAL

JANUARY 4th—I am fifteen today. My dear father called me into the Oak Parlour last evening, and gave me this book. He says he thinks I am old enough now to begin to keep a journal; it seems a little difficult to know how this ought to be done, but my father says if I write quite simply about everything that goes on it will soon become easy. After all, no one will look at my journal, it is for myself alone, so I shall treat it as a friend and tell it all my secrets.

Certainly it is not very often that anything does happen to us now, but there was a time when each day brought with it events so strange and dreadful that the memory of them is written upon my heart and can never be effaced.

I think that, as Father says a journal is meant to be the record of one's life, I might begin by a description of all that happened to us four years ago; especially as nothing so wonderful is

ever likely to take place again. I was quite a
little girl, only eleven, when we left our dear
home, but every scene through which we passed
is framed in my mind like a picture.

I suppose first of all I ought to describe everybody: by everybody I mean all those I love best
—my father, my mother, and my only brother
Louis, who is three years younger than I am.
It is impossible to write much about my father,
because when I think of him my heart feels too
full for words; indeed it seems to me that in all
the world there is no one else so noble and so
good.

I can remember that four years ago Mother
looked quite young and beautiful. Beautiful she
will always seem to me, but she is sadly changed
now. Her hair is touched with gray, and she is
very frail, with a sad look in her eyes, as though
she were haunted by the sorrows of the past.
She never complains, however, and she lives for
us and for the poor people in the village, who
adore her, and who come to her in all their
troubles. Her chief anxiety is about Louis, my
darling brother. He is very handsome, and we
are all proud of his great blue eyes and his golden
curls and grand air. He is very delicate, being
subject to strange fits of unconsciousness if suddenly alarmed or startled, which leave him weak
and suffering for days. This trouble too came
from the events of which I must now write, for
how could any story of our lives be complete
without an account of them?

In looking back I seem to feel again the soft
air of one beautiful September afternoon, when

I suppose I must have escaped from Nurse, for I remember finding myself alone in the Yew-tree Walk, where the beauty of everything and the happiness of living suddenly came upon me. I think it must have been because of all that happened on this wonderful day that I am able to recall my feelings so clearly. I can remember looking at our dear home with an affection I had never felt before, as I stood watching the sunbeams glancing on each gabled roof. From these my eyes wandered to the garden, which was lying in full sunshine, all ablaze with autumn flowers, while the stone lions on the steps which lead to the terrace were in deep shadow. Then I looked up at our yew-trees that are cut into curious shapes, and in which Father takes great pride. The one representing a lady in a hooped petticoat had just been freshly clipped, and appeared so natural that I remember pitying it from the bottom of my heart for having to stand there always. At this moment I remembered that Nurse might be wondering what had become of me, and I turned to look at the sundial that stands at the further end of the walk. I then saw that my father and mother were sitting on a stone seat beside it, and were so deep in conversation that they had not observed me. I can remember everything about them, even how they were dressed. Father wore a coat of crimson silk, with soft lace ruffles, and Mother's hair was powdered. She had on her pink satin gown, and she looked just as she does in her picture that hangs in the hall. It did not surprise me to see them so gaily attired, as I knew they had received some grand gentlemen from foreign parts that day at dinner. What did astonish me was to see the eager way in which Father was talking to Mother and holding her hand. I stood still gazing at them for a few moments, until I saw Mother turn away her head and burst into tears. I had never seen dear Mother so distressed before, and for a second I could not move. My heart ached in sympathy with her, and I was just going to run to her and throw my arms round her neck, when I recollected myself. I felt, in my childish fashion, that I was intruding upon a scene that was not meant for me, and I crept silently away. As I crossed the garden all the beauty seemed to have gone out of the day, and I felt afraid. What I feared I could not have told, but I thought it must indeed be something very dreadful that could make Mother cry. I longed to be with Nurse and Louis, and I was hastening up the great staircase, which is the shortest way to the nursery, when I was met by Grandmother's maid, who told me she had been looking for me everywhere, as her lady wished to see me. She would not suffer me to go to Nurse to be made tidy, but hastily removing my hood and smoothing my hair, she bade me come at once.

Dear Grandmother was in the Oak Parlour. I wish I could make a picture of her sitting there in her high-backed chair, with her silver hair and her soft lace cap, and her hands lying folded in her lap; for though her spinning-wheel was near her she had pushed it a little aside. Her face was quite calm, but I fancied she looked strangely at me as I made my curtsy, and she bade me come and take a seat beside her. For a few moments she was silent, then she spoke, and I can recall every word as if it were yesterday instead of four years ago.

"Marie," she said, "I have some solemn words to speak to you today. Your father has at length decided to take you all away to France. It will be a long and toilsome journey, and, by what folks say, strange events are taking place on the other side of the water; but, child, your father knows best, and though it grieves me sore that you should go, I must not repine."

My breath was almost taken away by these words.

"Go away to France, Grandmother?" I repeated.

"I forgot, my child, that you have as yet heard nothing," she answered. "You know, however, that your father's father was a French Noble, who was most unjustly banished from his country, and that, on coming to England, his mother's native land, he took her name of Hamilton and has always lived in this house."

"Yes, Grandmother," I said, when she paused.

She then went on to tell me that the present King of France had heard my father's story, and had sent to bid him return to France and the court, and to resume his father's title and take possession of his estates.

"It will be a hard parting, Marie," she said after a moment's silence, "but the Lord knows best. Try to be a comfort to your mother, my child. Whatever happens—and I fear much you are going among a strange heathenish people—do your duty, and fear God."

Grandmother spoke very solemnly. I felt inclined to cry, but I only whispered that I would try to do as she bade me, and, as she leaned forward to kiss me, the door opened and my father entered, leading my mother by the hand. They did not see me, I think, for they walked straight to Grandmother and knelt down before her.

"Mother, give us your blessing," they said, and she bowed her head and answered as she touched them with trembling hands, "The Lord bless you, my children, and bring you back in peace."

Then I stole away unnoticed, and went quickly to our own part of the house, but I paused outside the nursery. I could scarcely take in what I had heard. We were actually going away, and to France! the country of which I had so often heard my father speak, and whose strange tongue he loved to teach me. I now remembered how much less I had been with my mother than was usual during the past few weeks; also that there had been a great deal of mysterious coming and going, and that Nurse had been cross when I asked her about a mounted messenger I had seen coming up the avenue. This reminded me of my long absence from the nursery, and I quickly opened the door and went in. Louis was standing looking out of the window, and Nurse was spinning at her wheel. Nurse did not speak when I entered, but I saw that her eyes were red as if she had been crying. Louis ran to me and begged me to tell him what was the matter and why everyone was weeping. I put my arms round his neck and told him all I knew, but when Nurse broke in angrily, saying that her lady whom she had nursed in her arms, and her mistress Marie, and her master Louis, were to be taken away to a wicked country where they worshiped idols, and spoke bad words of the King, and ate abominable things, he grew frightened, and ran from me to her. I reminded her that France was our father's country, but she would not be silenced; and when Louis clung to her, saying if we went she must come too, she shook her head and said she was too old to change and to go among those fine godless folk. My mother's French maid was to go with us, she said, while she must bide at home and pray that the Lord might preserve us.

Upon this we all fell to weeping together, until Nurse remembered that it was our bedtime and dried her eyes. She got us our posset for supper with her own hands, but I, at least, had no heart to eat. Grandmother's words kept ringing in my ears; I felt as if I had suddenly become quite old with a serious duty before me, and I remember saying over and over to myself, "I must try to comfort Mother," until I fell asleep.

Then I dreamt that I stood again alone in the Yew-tree Walk, and that as I gazed at the figure of the lady, she suddenly stepped down and stood beside me. I saw that she was dressed not in leaves but in green satin, and that she had small bright eyes. She laughed at my surprise and said, "Silly child! silly child! you pity me! Ah! life is not all good, and it is quiet here. But you will see, you will see." She laughed again and laid her finger on her lips, then, bending forward and touching me, she whispered in my ear, "You must be a brave child if you would help your mother." There followed a rustling noise, and all the strange figures in the Yew-tree Walk began to laugh softly in a curious fashion which sounded like the murmuring of leaves. I thought I was in an enchanted place, and I was struggling in vain to move when I felt someone kiss me. I looked up, and found that I was in my own bed, with Mother bending over me.

"My darling, what is the matter?" she whispered as I opened my eyes.

"Nothing, nothing," I said eagerly, remembering I must not trouble her, but help her; "but Mother, I want to be a comfort to you."

Mother smiled. "My Marie has always been a comfort to me," she said, bidding me lie still, and saying that she would sit with me till I slept. After this I was not afraid or unhappy any more, for I thought that wherever we went she and our father would always be with us, therefore what could there be to fear?

CHAPTER III

A JOURNEY TO LONDON A HUNDRED YEARS AGO

I CAN tell very little about the next few days, and I have but a confused remembrance of many sad faces and hurried leave-takings; of Mother and Grandmother, outwardly calm, but hardly speaking, and looking wistfully at one another; of Father, watching them both with anxious eyes, trying in a hundred ways to help and cheer them.

At last the morning of our departure arrived. How well I remember it! We rose almost before it was light, for we were to start early in order to reach our first halting-place before nightfall. Nurse would let no one dress us but herself, and the tears were pouring down her face as she kept repeating, "Eh! but Mistress Marie darling, it is for the last time—the last time."

Neither Louis nor I could touch the breakfast she set before us, and it was quite a relief when she took us, one in each hand, and led us down to the dining-room where Father and Mother and Grandmother were. I think they could not trust themselves to speak, for Mother only kissed us, and then pressed Nurse's hand. She was already wrapped in her cloak, and her face was nearly covered by her hood, but I could see that her eyes too were red with weeping.

We had hardly been in the room a minute before old John came to the door and said in a trembling voice that the carriage had come, and all was ready.

"My children, you must not delay," said dear Grandmother, as she took her gold-headed stick in her hand, and walked firmly into the hall, where the great door stood open, and where the servants were all gathered to bid us farewell. Mother took Father's arm and followed, Nurse hung back, and Louis seemed quite bewildered, but he let me take his hand, and when I whispered to him not to cry for Mother's sake he kept his tears back, and walked bravely by my side.

At the door Grandmother stopped. Her face was quite calm, but her hand shook as she laid it on Mother's head and kissed and blessed her. Then she kissed us all, and when it came to my turn she said, "Remember, Marie, you must be a comfort to your mother."

Some of the old servants who had known Mother all her life came crowding round us as we went to the carriage; but Nurse put them all aside, and with loud laments seized Louis, who clung to her and began to cry. It was more than poor Mother could bear; she covered her face with her hands, and Father placed her quickly in the carriage; then he took Louis gently but firmly from Nurse, and put him on Mother's lap. I followed, and the man and the maid got into the rumble. Then Father lifted his hat and bowed low to Grandmother, whose figure framed by the doorway formed a picture long remembered by us all.

"My good people, farewell," he said to the servants, who were crowding round, then he stepped in, the postillions cracked their whips, the carriage began to move, and we were off!

Away we went down the avenue and through the village street, where, though it was so early, many of the cottagers were standing waiting to wish us "God speed" on our long, long journey. The women curtsied as we passed, and the men stood with their heads uncovered, and many a blessing was poured on Louis and on me. Father and I, I remember, leaned out of the carriage and acknowledged these kindly greetings as best we might, for Mother was too much distressed to look up.

I was straining my eyes to catch a last glimpse of our dear home from the top of the hill just outside the village, when I noticed how weary Mother looked, and Louis, who had fallen asleep, was resting his head on her arm. I made up a little bed on the seat beside me with some wraps, and ventured to ask whether he might not lie there with his head on my lap. Father gave me an approving glance, and lifted Louis, who never stirred, and placed him on the little couch I had made. Then Mother leaned back wearily, and presently she too slept. I, on the contrary, far from being drowsy, felt intensely wide awake. In spite of my grief at leaving dear Grandmother, and the place we loved so well, and the old servants, I was full of excitement. Hitherto my longest journey had been to our nearest town, which is only seven miles distant from home. Now I was going far away over the sea, to see strange new places and Father's country, of which I had so often heard him speak. I longed to ask him all about it, but he sat silent, apparently thinking deeply, and of course it was impossible for me to interrupt his thoughts by my questions.

At last I suppose he noticed my longing looks, for he smiled at me, and asked if it grieved me very much to leave our English home.

I tried to tell him what I felt, and then, seeing an anxious look on his face, I said, "*I* am not afraid, Father. Nurse has frightened Louis a little by telling him that we shall never return, but I know we shall be quite safe with you."

Father smiled and patted my head. "Well said, my child," he answered. "Never fear anything except dishonour." These were his very words, and they sank into my heart never to be forgotten. He then went on to say that as I had such a brave heart he would tell me as much of the reasons for our journey as he thought I could understand. He said that though he had been very young when his father was banished from France he had never forgotten that he was a Frenchman. The present King had graciously remembered him, and, wishing to repair the wrong that had been done to his father, had invited him to return to take up the old name and title, and to serve his majesty. My father went on to say that had he consulted his own feelings he might have hesitated about accepting the offer. He had, however, not only the honour of a Noble name to consider, but also his service to the King. It was rumoured that troubles threatened his majesty, which rendered it the duty of his faithful subjects to rally round him. Therefore we were setting out in all haste, and Father said he had no fear in taking us, as his majesty had graciously promised Mother a place in the Queen's household.

"And what is our new name, Father?" I asked when he had finished speaking.

Father smiled again. "I am the Comte de Grandville," he said; "and you will be Mademoiselle de Grandville, and Louis will be the Vicomte de Grandville."

At this I laughed outright, thinking how funny it would be to be called by such grand names, and what strange mistakes we should sometimes make. Then I remembered Grandmother and our home, and I asked sadly if we were never to go back again.

Father told me that he hoped we should go back for a visit very soon, but that our home was henceforth to be in France. I suppose he saw my eyes fill up with tears when he said this, and again his very words come back to me almost as if they had been spoken yesterday.

"My Marie," he said gently, "if we would find happiness in this world we must go where duty calls, and be loyal and patient even though things seem hard; young as you are, I know you will be brave for your mother's sake and mine."

I can remember how I forced back my tears as Father bent to kiss me, thinking how great and noble he was, and that there could be no one else like him in the world.

Soon after this, I think, we changed horses, and then Louis woke up and we amused ourselves by looking out of the windows and watching the new scenes through which we passed. I have but a faint remembrance of the inn at which we stopped to dine, but I can recollect quite distinctly that just as we were starting off again we heard the winding of a horn, and the mail-coach dashed into the courtyard. I remember how amused and interested Louis and I were in watching the townspeople gathering round, eager for news, and in seeing the odd, muffled figures that got down from the coach. We had never before seen so large a town, and we were very sorry to leave it behind and drive once more along the country roads, where we met only a few village folk.

Only one more incident of our journey is firmly impressed on my mind.

I think we must have been traveling two or three days when some slight accident happened to one of the wheels of our carriage. I recollect Father seemed much annoyed at the necessary delay, and the moment it was repaired we hurried on faster than ever. Father would eat no dinner when we stopped in the middle of the day, but kept pacing up and down the inn parlour with his watch in his hand, while we hastily swallowed some hot soup. Directly the horses were changed we set off again, and Father impatiently waved aside the host—who stepped up to us just as we were starting—saying we were pressed for time, as he wished to pass Thornton Heath before dark. But the good man would not be silenced. "If your honour would condescend to listen to me," he said, "I would pray you not to cross the Heath except by broad daylight. It is not so very long since his majesty's mail was attacked and robbed there."

"Thanks, thanks!" said Father; "tell them to drive on."

The postillions cracked their whip, and we went off once more. The man's mysterious words haunted me. What did he mean? I had heard Nurse talk of highwaymen, could it be that—? I shivered and closed my eyes and presently fell asleep. It was quite dark when I was suddenly aroused and found that we had stopped at a small wayside inn, and that Father was anxiously inquiring whether they could give us lodging there for the night. On being told that this was impossible, as a great fair was being held in the neighbourhood and the inn was quite full, he looked at Mother and said, "The Heath is dangerous, but we have no choice. We must go on."

Mother glanced at us. Louis was sleeping soundly; I sat quite still and closed my eyes. "Certainly we must go on," she said calmly.

"On, then!" cried Father to the postillions, "and double pay if we pass safely over the Heath." I looked out and saw that we were crossing a wild desolate moorland. My heart beat fast as I saw Father grasp his pistols. In perfect silence, the horses floundering along the heavy road, on we went. Once there came the sound of galloping behind us, and a man on horseback dashed past our carriage at full speed. Father's face grew stern and more anxious; Mother sat quite still, with her eyes fixed on us. Gradually the road improved, the desolate moorland faded out of sight, and we reached a small village amongst pleasant country lanes, and saw some flickering lights in the distance.

"Where are we?" Father shouted from the window.

"Close to the Oxford Road," answered the men.

"Dear husband, we are safe," said Mother as he put his pistols aside. "The first stage of our journey is complete. Let us take it as a good sign for the days to come."

CHAPTER IV

ON THE ROAD TO VERSAILLES

THAT night we rested safely in London, but the great city, with its noise and bustle, has left little impression on my memory. Very indistinctly I remember another hurried journey, then a dark angry-looking sea, and a vessel in which we embarked at dead of night. When I awoke next morning we were lying at anchor, and I heard Father talking cheerfully of the favouring wind that had carried us across.

A few more days must have gone by, and then, like a vision, a very different scene rises before me.

We were in Paris, with its narrow streets and high houses. The sky overhead was blue, and there was a lightness in the air that made one's heart dance with a sense of joy.

The King, having heard of our arrival, had sent to bid us come to Versailles to be presented to

their majesties, and we were ready to set out.
Mother was looking lovely in a beautiful court
dress with a long train, and she wore diamonds
round her neck and in her hair. Louis seemed
prettier than ever in a blue satin coat trimmed
with broad lace. The ruffles round his wrists
almost covered his small hands, and a miniature
sword with a gold hilt hung by his side. I had
on a little court dress too. It was of pink satin,
and my hair was powdered, which made me feel
very strange, and I had diamond buckles in my
shoes.

Presently, with a great noise and clatter, the
carriage that was to convey us to the King's
palace dashed up to the door of our hotel. It
was one of the court carriages; the postillions
wore a livery of scarlet and gold, and the har-
ness was mounted with pure gold. Within, the
linings were of soft white satin, wrought with
silver fleurs-de-lis.

Quite a little crowd assembled to see us start,
but instead of smiling at us, as our poor people
at home used to do, they looked fierce and sullen,
and muttered strangely. I fancied that they
were angry with us because we were English,
and I felt a little frightened, but when I recollected that Father was now the Comte de Grandville I smiled at my fears and thought how
Mother would soon teach them to love us.

The streets were narrow and ill-paved, and
there was no footway, yet we drove very rapidly,
scattering as we went the groups of people who
stood about idly. Often there was barely time
for the mothers to snatch their little children

from beneath the horses' feet, but our postillions, cracking their whips loudly, dashed right on regardless of all risks.

I could not help noticing the bitter looks of the poor pinched faces of the bystanders, as their eyes followed our grand carriage. I saw that Father and Mother were anxious and troubled, and at last Mother could bear it no longer, but begged Father to bid the riders go more slowly until we were beyond the city.

Just as she spoke the horses were pulled up with such a sudden jerk that Louis and I were thrown quite out of our seats. Loud cries followed, and Father let down the window to see what had happened.

"It is nothing, monseigneur," said a footman, coming forward; "only a moment's entanglement with the horses of another carriage which was crossing monseigneur's way. No harm is done; we can proceed at once."

But I had been looking out of the opposite window, and I had seen a sight which I shudder even now to remember. With a smothered cry a strange, wild-looking man had rushed among the struggling horses and shouting footmen, and, stooping down, had raised in his arms the apparently lifeless form of a little girl. He rested her white face tenderly on his shoulder, and as he passed he disengaged one arm for a second and shook his fist at our carriage with a terrible expression on his fierce countenance. All this happened in a moment. Mother was looking the other way, but I called out to her immediately to show her what had taken place. She turned, and her face grew pale as she saw a little crutch lying near us in the road and the figure of a man moving slowly away with his burden.

"Quick!" she cried to the servant, "bring that man here. A child is hurt; we must get help."

"Here, fellow!" called out the servant without moving, "Madame deigns to desire to speak to you."

The man took no heed, he only moved off a little more quickly, while the people standing round began to mutter angrily. Father had not seen all that we had, and being, no doubt, anxious for our safety, said hastily that as he feared we could do no good we had better drive on.

But I had seen the child's white face, with its pinched, hungry look, and my heart ached with pity for her. I felt we could not leave her thus, and I clasped my hands and implored him to make an effort to help her.

Father advanced his head and looked out. At this moment the man laid down the little girl near a fountain, dashed his hat into the water, and sprinkled some over her face, calling out wildly, "My child dies!—is killed!"

"My good people," said Mother much agitated, "here is gold. Go and get help." But no one moved to take the gold.

Then I jumped up. "Let me go to her," I said. Without waiting for an answer I took two gold pieces in my hand and sprang from the carriage. The people fell back—I knew they were not bad, only their hearts were aching for the little girl— and I went straight to where she lay and knelt down beside her. As I did so she opened her eyes, and seeing me bending over her she said gently, "Is this an angel? Is it Paradise?"

"No, no, not an angel; only a friend who wants to make you better," I whispered; but I spoke in English, forgetting that she could not understand me. I saw she looked bewildered, almost frightened, so I stooped and kissed her, and then she smiled faintly. My court dress was touching her little threadbare cotton gown; I felt almost ashamed of my fine clothes, and as the dreadful contrast between her life and mine struck me the tears rolled down my cheeks. Seeing this she put up her little thin hand and touched me lovingly. At this moment I looked up, and saw her father, who was watching us closely. He moved a little forward, his fierce eyes actually dim with tears, and taking off his cap he muttered something that I could not quite understand, but I think he said that I had a good heart, and was not like those others. I saw, however, that though he spoke roughly he did not mean to be unkind, so I smiled at him, and, putting the money into the child's hand, whispered to her how grieved we were that she had been hurt, and that Mother wanted her to buy something to make her better. Seeing only a look of wonder in her eyes, I suddenly remembered that she could not understand a word I said. In my excitement I had nearly forgotten how to speak the French tongue at all, but I managed to say brokenly, "I should like very much to come and see you. Will you tell me your name?"

"My name is Toinette," she answered, fixing her dark eyes on my face.

"Toinette, Toinette," I repeated, "I will be sure to remember. Adieu, Toinette!"

Father, who had followed me, now took my arm and bade me return to the carriage. On our way back the people smiled at us; and the mothers told their little ones to kiss their hands to "the little mademoiselle." They raised a cheer as we drove off, and Mother kissed me, and said I had done quite right in trying to help the poor child.

I then asked if we might not seek her out in her own home; but when I said that I only knew her name was Toinette, Mother shook her head sadly, saying she feared it would be impossible to find her. Father, seeing my distress, patted me on the head, and said that I did not understand. Paris was a big place, and there were many children living there of that name.

"But none just like her," I urged, and he said we might try to trace her, but he feared we should not succeed.

I could scarcely believe it then, but I found that my father was right. Paris was not like our village, and to look for "Toinette" among its multitudes, was as hopeless a task as to search a needle in a bundle of hay.

CHAPTER V

AT THE KING'S PALACE

AFTER this we drove on in silence for a long time.
Father and Mother were busy with their own
thoughts. I could not forget Toinette's white
pitiful face, and Louis, who had been terrified at
seeing me go among the angry people, and who
had with difficulty been prevented from following
me, sat quite still holding my hand as if determined not to let me go again.

I can so well remember the dreary road in the
midst of a sandy plain, bordered on each side by
gray poplars, along which we drove after we left
Paris. Then suddenly the scene changed; we entered gardens that seemed to belong to Fairy-
land; in the distance there arose a palace that
looked like a city. Fountains were playing in
the sunshine, tossing up sparkling jets of spray;
on every side were stately avenues, and countless
yew-trees, cut into shapes far more curious and
exact in form than those at our home, sprang
from the wide green lawns, or stood like sentinels
along the borders of the drives.

The sight of the yew-trees delighted us. Louis clapped his hands, and even Mother smiled and looked happier than she had done for many a day.

In the meantime gay carriages, filled with beautifully dressed ladies and grand gentlemen, were dashing past us. Everyone seemed happy and light-hearted. This was like another world, and it was difficult to believe that only a few leagues separated us from Toinette and the poor hungry people.

When we reached the palace two footmen in gorgeous liveries of scarlet and gold came out to open the carriage-door, and we were conducted by them up a magnificent marble staircase. It was, we were told, a fête day, and the palace seemed alive with servants, pages in splendid dresses of velvet and silk, and gentlemen in waiting, whose brilliantly coloured coats were sewn with jewels. At the top of the grand staircase an officer came forward, and bowing low, said, "Monsieur le Comte, his majesty desires me to receive and welcome you. You and Madame la Comtesse will be presented to their majesties when dinner is over."

Father bowed to this grand gentleman, who went on talking, and he spoke so clearly and distinctly that I could understand every word.

"You and I, Monsieur de Grandville," he said, "should not meet as strangers. We shall be neighbours in fair Touraine; our fathers fought side by side more than once, and it is for these reasons that his majesty has graciously commanded me to receive you, and to welcome you back to our country, from which you have been absent too long."

So saying he bowed lower than ever, and. offered his arm to Mother, whom I scarcely knew as Madame la Comtesse de Grandville. People looked at us curiously as we went on to one of the anterooms, there to await the return of the King and Queen from the great dining-hall to their own apartments. A good many of the courtiers who were standing about came forward to be presented to Mother and Father, and they noticed us kindly. Louis' long golden curls attracted the admiration of these fine ladies with their powdered hair. They went into raptures over his beauty; in fact they praised us both so much and so openly that I felt shy and clung to Mother, leaving Louis, who did not understand half they said, and whose cheeks were flushed with excitement, to enjoy all their caresses and bon-bons. And now a rustling sound of silk and satin was heard in the distance, and everyone became attentive and expectant, as a double door which led into a corridor was thrown open by two servants, and a glittering train appeared. First came some pages and ushers, and then the centre of all eyes in that brilliant throng, the King and Queen.

Apart from his gorgeous array, his coat sewn with diamonds, his frills of richest lace, one might not perhaps have thought the King very different from other men; but the Queen, even if dressed as a peasant, would still have looked a Queen. As she walked slowly forward, carrying her beautiful head erect, it was not her jewels, nor her train of gold brocade that fixed one's attention, but her majestic mien. When they had advanced a few steps into the anteroom they paused. Then the gentleman who had met us on our arrival came forward, and, motioning to Father and Mother to follow him, he announced their names.

Upon this Father and Mother advanced and knelt before their majesties, who raised them kindly. The King spoke some gracious words of welcome which I could not quite hear, and after he had done speaking he sighed, and would have passed on, but the Queen stopped him.

"One moment," she said in a voice clear as a bell; "where are the little English children?" Mother glanced at me; trembling very much, I took Louis' hand and led him forward, and knelt down before their majesties. The King laid his hand kindly on Louis' head, and, encouraged by this, I dared to lift my eyes. There was a beautiful tender look on the Queen's face that banished all my fear, and raising us she kissed us both.

"Your children are charming," she said to Mother. "I hope I shall often see them. Your little girl shall talk English to my daughter."

Then, with a gracious bend of her stately head, she passed on with the King, and with all their glittering train. Our beautiful Queen! we cherish as a sacred recollection her every word and gesture. From that hour I loved her, and I love her memory now. Alas! alas!

Father and Mother had been appointed to the household of the King and Queen, and a small set of rooms was set apart for us in the palace. Thither we now repaired. After a time of so much excitement Mother said she longed to spend a quiet evening with us. This, however, was impossible, as both she and Father were obliged to be present at a gay fête which was to be held that evening, so after a short rest Mother had only time to dress in haste before returning to the court. She kissed us both fondly as she said good-night; and then she knelt down with us, and prayed that God might watch over us and bless us in this strange new life.

It was not long before I fell asleep, but the Queen's beautiful face and Toinette's sad eyes haunted me and mingled strangely in my dreams.

At last I thought I was walking alone on the great marble staircase of the palace, when suddenly the figure of the lady in the Yew-tree Walk at home stood beside me. I was startled and perplexed, and asked her how she came there. For answer she touched me with a branch which she held in her hand, I was lifted off my feet and the next moment found myself standing in a long corridor whose windows overlooked the gardens. To my amazement I saw that all the yew-trees were kissing their hands and bowing, and I understood that these must be relations of our English yew-trees, which pleased and amused me very much. Just as I began to laugh, however, there seemed to come a sound of sobbing on the air, and I saw all the branches swaying themselves to and fro as if in grief. I turned round, and lo! the beautiful statues in the corridor were weeping and wringing their hands, and from the orange-trees and palms which stood on the staircase came a faint moan.

"What is it?" I said, "What is the matter? What can there be to cry for in this happy place where everyone is gay?" and in my dream my thoughts flew to Toinette. My strange companion spoke at last.

"How little you know—you human beings who think yourselves so wise! Pity yourselves— the Queen—not Toinette. Be brave and—" Terrified I awoke, and what struck me as the strangest part of my dream was, that I could have seen, even in my sleep, someone from our dear home, without asking how all whom we had left behind were faring.

CHAPTER VI

THE QUEEN'S TOILETTE

I MUST not linger over the short time that followed. Very, very short it was, and happy enough to us children, and I think Mother grew more reconciled to her life; but Father's face became graver and more anxious every day, and I have heard since that the gay courtiers were offended by his gravity and by the very serious advice which he gave the King. I almost shrink from the story I have to tell now. My pen seems far too weak and feeble to describe one half of the strange and awful events of which I must write.

Full well I remember a day that rose clear and bright with no sign to foretell the horrors with which it was to close. Mother and Louis and I walked in the gardens in the morning as was our custom. A long letter had just arrived from Grandmother, and we dwelt with delight on every little detail of home which she gave us. At its conclusion she said she hoped I would not forget her last charge to me. I knew what she meant. How little I thought that would be the last message I should receive from her for many a long day!

At the usual time Mother went to attend the Queen's toilette, and, on this occasion, her majesty sent for Louis and me soon afterwards.

I shut my eyes and I see the whole scene again.

Queen Marie Antoinette was seated at her dressing table, which was draped with lace and bright with mirrors, and all the articles of the toilette were mounted in chased gold. Her hair was dressed, and was being powdered; on one side stood a grand court lady, holding in her hand the simple muslin robe which the Queen loved to wear when no great ceremony was to take place; on the other side was Mother, holding a basin of pure gold for the Queen's use, while a third lady stood by with a richly trimmed towel. The greatest ladies of the court were seated on sofas round the room. Many people came and went, generals in full uniform, and gentlemen with grand names were announced, for this was the Queen's time of reception. She bowed to everyone who came in, to some she spoke a few words, but her face looked sad and anxious, and she inquired continually where the King was, and looked often towards the door as though she expected him to enter.

Presently there was a little stir in the room, everyone rose, and the Queen looked up eagerly, but it was only one of the royal princesses. Her majesty half-raised herself, an honour she only paid to those of royal blood, and Mother hastened to place the basin she held in the hands of an attendant, who gave it to the princess to hold for the Queen, for at the French court it was considered an honour even for those of the highest rank to serve their sovereign.

Mother fell back a little and looked towards a sofa on which Madame Royale and the Dauphin were seated with their governess, while Louis and I were standing beside them. I had been talking English, and trying to make them say the words properly, and we were all very merry together.

"Go to them, madame," I heard the Queen say— and we all love to record every word that fell from her lips—"it is good to hear such laughter. Let them play, their hearts will ache soon enough." She sighed deeply as she spoke, and went on after a moment's pause:

"This afternoon we will go to the Little Trianon. I will start at two; you, madame, and your children will accompany us."

Some of the great ladies looked rather disdainfully at Mother as she crossed the room to join us. I have since heard that they were jealous of the favour which the Queen bestowed on her. Mother says that in the midst of all her splendour Marie Antoinette had often sighed for a simple natural life, and that she would ask her many questions about our quiet village and our happy days at home. She says too, that when clouds were gathering round the throne, in spite of all the observance with which the Queen was surrounded, she scarcely knew friend from foe, even among those of her own household. I think if this was so it was little wonder she loved and trusted my mother, who would have died for her.

But to return to my story. When Mother came up to us the Dauphin took her hand and made her sit down beside him.

"Marie has been telling us of your home," he said; "but we cannot say your English words, they sound so droll."

"And we, monseigneur, find it hard to speak your charming French tongue," answered Mother.

"But madame has so much talent," returned the Dauphin with courtly grace. "She already speaks our language as though she had lived in France all her life."

"I *am* a Frenchman," cried Louis, "and I mean to speak French like monseigneur the Dauphin, whose servant I shall be."

While those around us were laughing at this little speech there was a stir in the room, for the Queen's toilette was finished; but before they could disperse a strange rumbling was heard.

"Is that thunder?" inquired the Queen, moving towards the door.

There was no answer, but all stood spell-bound, for, as I learnt afterwards, the courtiers knew full well the meaning of those awful sounds which no one who has once heard them can forget. It was the muttering thunder of an angry crowd rolling on in one direction. Above the rush and tumult and the trampling of many feet, could be heard the shrieks of women, and hoarse cries of men, sounds which increased in volume as they drew near; and told that soon the surging crowd would beset the palace doors.

The Queen stopped and her ladies looked at one another with pale terror-stricken faces; they dared not tell her what they feared.

At this moment the door was burst open, and an usher cried out wildly:

"Your majesty, the Paris mob is upon us!"

The certainty of danger seemed to calm the Queen. "Where is the King?" she asked.

"His majesty has just left his apartments and is in the mirror gallery," was the reply.

Taking the Dauphin in one hand, and Madame Royale in the other, Queen Marie Antoinette went to join him followed by her ladies. How vividly the scene that then met my wondering eyes returns with all its memories!

The King was standing by one of the windows of a gallery which overlooked the terraces, and a group of gentlemen in brilliant uniforms, their faces fierce and eager, and their hands on their swords, surrounded him. He looked annoyed, anxious and irresolute, and his hair and dress were in disorder.

He turned as the Queen took her place beside him. It was a terrible scene—a sea of white faces maddened with fury; rough hands brandishing all sorts of weapons; women with streaming hair and blood-shot eyes, mingling amongst the men and urging them on. From one and all rose the fierce cry, "Bread! bread!" There were other words, threats, imprecations, wild utterances of fury and despair. Never could the Queen have heard such words before—never, never could she have beheld such a scene, and yet she stood calm and resolute, for danger had nerved her proud courageous heart.

"Sire!" she said turning to the King, "you will order your guards to disperse this rabble?"

"No, no," said the King, "blood might be shed, the blood of my people! We will hear what they desire."

The Queen seemed impatient, while the King having opened one of the windows went out on the balcony and presented himself to the people.

"To Paris! to Paris!" shouted the mob, and called for the Queen, who stepped out calm and proud, and for a moment there was silence; her beauty and her majesty had touched the hearts of the fickle crowd. It was only for an instant; a woman's voice was uplifted in menace, another and another followed, and soon the whole crowd burst out into threats and insults.

"Down with the Austrian; throw us out the Jezebel! Death to kings! Bread! Bread for the starving people!"

Marie Antoinette stood before them undaunted. A voice in the crowd cried: "The children, bring out the children!" Then the first tremor ran through the Queen's frame, and her pale lips quivered. She hesitated for an instant: a thousand voices took up the cry, "The children! the children!"

"Let her majesty deign to gratify her people," said a pale-faced courtier in the gallery, and Madame Royale and the Dauphin, who were trying to emulate their mother's firmness, came out of their own accord and stood on either side of her.

Then followed a momentary lull: I suppose

there were mothers and fathers in the crowd, and the sight of the Queen standing calmly before them between her children must have touched them, but not for long. Those behind pressed heavily on those in front, the doors of the palace yielded to their rush, some of the King's guards were slain, in a few moments the tumultuous crowd were surging through the palace, bringing ruin and destruction everywhere.

The Queen left the balcony; a few of the most devoted of her friends, among whom were Father and Mother, to whom Louis and I were clinging, hurried her to one of the great reception-rooms and drew a heavy table in front of her and her children; some of the ladies hid themselves, whilst the King held parley with the foremost of the rabble.

"You shall have bread," he said; "I will send out provisions to the gardens, and if you desire it I will return with you to Paris. I am my people's father, and I only wish their good."

His words were repeated from mouth to mouth, and shouts of acclamation filled the air. "To Paris! to Paris! The King goes to Paris! Now we shall have bread, we, and our little ones!"

The King ordered his chariot to be prepared, and sent a message to the Queen. "His good people wished to see him in Paris. Would her majesty be ready to join him in an hour?"

None who saw it could ever forget the look on the Queen's face during that terrible hour of waiting. Our brave mother, whilst we still clung to her, stood close beside her royal mistress, and when the Queen's carriage was announced she knelt before her.

"Her majesty," she said, "will permit us to accompany her?"

"Alas! madame," said the Queen bitterly, "I can permit no longer. I grieve that we should have brought you to this ill-fated country. Return to your happy English home."

"At this moment of danger," answered Mother, "I think no more of my English home. I wish only to serve your majesty."

A tear glistened in the Queen's eyes and her proud face softened.

"Madame," she said, "you are not wise to attatch yourself to the unfortunate, and it is my bitter fate to bring misfortune to those that love me. Be persuaded, and return to England while you may."

"Never, your majesty," said another voice. It was our father who spoke, who, having been dismissed from his service on the King, was seeking us. "We will not return while I have one drop of blood with which to defend the honour of my Queen."

Marie Antoinette rose as she saw the King advancing to lead her to the carriage, and presented her hand to Father, who kissed it with the deepest reverence, then with kind looks of farewell to us all, for I think she could not trust herself to speak, she walked calmly down the marble staircase, and bade a last goodbye to all the glories of Versailles.

The courtiers were now all eager to depart, some to their country homes, some to make arrangements for leaving France, and a faithful

few, determined as my father was, to follow the
King to Paris to help him if they could. By this
time, however, the whole palace was at the mercy
of the mob, and it was with the greatest difficulty
that we could find a small carriage to convey us
to Paris. It was brought to a back entrance,
and we were creeping down a small staircase,
when a door on the landing above was burst
open, and a woman's shrill voice cried, "Here
are some of the aristocrats stealing away!" In-
stantly the staircase was filled with grotesque
and ragged figures. A woman seized Louis, who
screamed loudly and clung to Mother.

"Let the little cub go," cried a man, shaking
her by the arm. Father's eyes flashed, and he
laid his hand on his sword; at this moment a
tall man with red eyes and blackened face pushed
himself to the front. Disguised as he was I
recognized him at once.

"That is Toinette's father," I cried. "Oh! my
good sir, save us, save us!"

The man paused, gazed at us for a few minutes,
and then passed his hand over his eyes.

"Hold!" he said, as the crowd over whom he
seemed to possess some authority fell back. "This
is my affair, a private vengeance that I have vowed
to carry out. Leave these aristocrats to me."

This was a language the crowd understood.
They rushed up the narrow staircase laughing
hideously. "Ah! we will leave them to our
Jacques," cried one and all.

The man whom they called Jacques was meantime hurrying us into the carriage. I was far too
frightened to say a word, but as he laid his hand

on my arm to help me in I raised my eyes to his face. He took off his red cap of liberty and said, "For your sake, little mademoiselle, for your sake."

"I think our Marie has saved us," said Father, kissing me as we drove away.

My brain was whirling. I felt as though what had passed must be some fearful dream. Yet through it all there came to me a throb of pleasure, as I knew I had won my father's approval.

CHAPTER VII

MONSIEUR JACQUES

I WILL pass quickly over the sad and dreary days that followed our removal to Paris. Father took a small lodging near the palace, but he and Mother were soon dismissed from their service on the King and Queen, who were no longer able to choose their own attendants, and whose palace became in reality their prison.

Of the terrible events which were taking place almost daily we children did not often hear, for our parents did not wish to make our lives sad and unhappy, and carefully guarded us from all knowledge of their fears for the future. We lived very simply and frugally, not only because any display would have been dangerous, but because, as I have since learnt, Father was devoting all his money to the King's cause, which he still hoped might triumph.

Very soon after we were settled in Paris M. Jacques found us out. He came one day and told Mother in his rough fashion that Louis and

I might go through the streets in safety, as we were under his protection. At that time Mother was almost tempted to smile at this remark, but she replied gravely, and took the opportunity of thanking him for the service he had rendered us.

"The people of France, madame, do not desire to injure the *innocent*," he said, glancing at Louis and me as he moved impatiently to the door. Mother stopped him, begging him to tell us of Toinette, and whether her hurt had been serious.

"Not serious, madame," he answered, still angry and impatient. When Mother went on to say that I longed to see his little girl, of whom we had often spoken, he looked at her as though astonished to hear such words from her lips. His face softened, however, and he said if the little mademoiselle really wished to see his child she might do so. He then gave us an address and various directions by which we might find our way to where he lived, adding, as he bowed and left the room, "You will do well to pause, madame, before you bring *your* child to see how *ours* live."

There was a look of inexpressible bitterness on his face which I could not understand. I wondered if he was really as bad as the rest of the dreadful people. I have since learnt to wonder whether they were bad at all, or only maddened by their wrongs. This, however, is a secret I can only confide to my book as I hasten on with my story.

The next day Mother and I set out alone on foot in search of M. Jacques' abode, for Father thought that we should be safer unattended.

After many wanderings we found ourselves in the most miserable part of the great city, among narrow streets where open gutters were filled with foul refuse of every sort. By the side of these black streams little children with hungry faces played, whilst women, haggard and fierce of look, sat knitting at their doors.

They stared at us, and Mother glanced nervously at me, reproaching herself, I am sure, for having yielded to my entreaties and brought me to such a place. One of the women stepped up to us rudely as if to accost us. Mother, however, before she could speak, inquired in a calm voice if she could assist us to find the dwelling of one M. Jacques.

"Jacques!" screamed the woman, "our Jacques!" and immediately half a dozen others rushed forward eager to guide us, smiling and civil. The very name of M. Jacques appeared to act as a talisman. We could not understand it then.

Soon we turned into a courtyard, and after ascending many dark flights of broken stone steps we came to a door, at which we knocked. The voice of M. Jacques bade us enter. We found a poor, bare room, with no fire burning, though the day was cold. M. Jacques was alone, and he rose courteously as we entered, glancing with surprise at Mother, who was almost exhausted by our long walk and her anxiety.

"The very sight of these wretched places overwhelms madame," he said bitterly, placing a chair for her, and still standing himself. Mother smiled a little, though I could see that this strange man alarmed her.

"I am not unaccustomed to go among the poor, and I know something of their sorrows," she said gently. "May we not see your little girl?" she went on, as he did not reply.

"She is in the next room—in bed—where she often lies now," he answered. "Mademoiselle may go to her when she wakes."

"Is she your only child?" inquired Mother.

"Madame," he said, his face working strangely, "she is all I have in the world except—my wrongs."

There was an awful look in his eyes as he spoke. I grew frightened, and, creeping close to Mother, took her hand. Just then a feeble voice from the next room called "Father." He rose immediately, his whole expression changed and softened. Holding out his hand to me he said, "Come with me and thou shalt see Toinette."

Mother looked at me, and I understood that I must go alone. Trembling very much, I followed M. Jacques to the inner chamber, where, though everything was very poor and bare, there was more show of comfort. There was a small wood fire on the hearth, and on the bed, propped up by pillows lay Toinette. Her face had that old, weary look which belongs to those who have never known health, her eyes were half-closed, and her voice was feeble as she said, "Is that thou, my father?"

He smiled at her tenderly and moved a little aside, disclosing me. She gazed at me as if she saw a vision.

"The little lady has come to see thee," he said.

"I told thee she had a good heart and would not forget."

I now went forward. "I have thought of you often and often," I said, "and longed to help you. Are you better? Were you much hurt?"

"You cried because I suffered pain," said the child not heeding my questions. "You are of the angels, but where are your shining clothes?"

"You must love me without them," I said, stooping to kiss her, "for I don't think I shall ever wear such lovely clothes again."

"The little mademoiselle does not need fine clothes to make her lovely," said M. Jacques going to the door and leaving us alone.

For a little while we sat silent, hand in hand, but before long we began to talk, and I found that Toinette had been a little sufferer all her life. Her simple story was soon told, but we had still a great deal to say to one another, when I remembered that I must not delay too long, and I parted from her, promising to come again as soon as possible

That was the beginning of my acquaintance with Toinette. I soon grew to love her dearly, and I used to go to her once every week. Mother never went with me again, for M. Jacques would fetch me and bring me home. He did not speak much on our journeys to and fro; but he was always kind and careful. The roughest people would remove their red caps when they saw me with him, and though Mother used to tremble when I set out, I think Father was not afraid to trust him.

A year or more went by. Things grew worse and worse. At last there came a day which is too horrible even to remember. I try to blot it from my memory.

The King was no longer king, even in name. There was no hope, nothing could be done, and I think for our sakes Father would have returned to England, but it was too late; he was not allowed to leave the country.

We were sitting sadly at dinner one day in spring. It was dull and gloomy, and a keen east wind was blowing. I was not well, and Mother said that it was a pity I should be obliged to go and see Toinette that afternoon. Dear Father looked at me anxiously, remarking that it would not do to offend M. Jacques, when, almost as he spoke, we heard a noise outside, the door was flung open, and M. Jacques himself, accompanied by some of the National Guard, entered the room. Louis screamed, Mother and I flew to Father, who rose and inquired the reason of this disturbance. M. Jacques did not answer, but addressing the soldiers and pointing to Father said, "I denounce this citizen, calling himself Comte de Grandville, as a traitor to the state." Immediately Father was seized and bound. No doubt he saw that resistance was useless, for he submitted quietly. In vain Mother and I wept and entreated M. Jacques and the cruel soldiers to have pity upon us. M. Jacques answered us not a word, and when Father was in custody he went on in an un-moved voice to denounce Louis, who had since the first moment been struggling bravely to be calm and who was standing a little apart with clenched hands as though he were tempted to try his feeble power against our tormentors. With a shriek he flew to Mother, who clasped him in her arms and in the most touching words, with tears streaming down her cheeks, begged to be allowed to go with him to prison. The rude soldiers only laughed and tore our darling from her, while M. Jacques watched them with a cruel smile and a strange faraway look in his eyes as though he did not see us. I knelt to him, I clung round his knees, calling to him and imploring him to aid us. At last he deigned to look at me, and still with that awful smile on his face, he bent and whispered, "Peace, child! Why should I pity you? Other mothers have suffered as yours does, and with as tender hearts."

His cruel words stung me, and I staggered to my feet. He touched me gently and said in a changed voice, "Courage! I will remember you and yours as you remembered Toinette."

With this he left us, and this was the only grain of comfort on which we had to subsist for days and months.

Oh! the long weary time that dragged slowly by after we lost Father and Louis. Not a word reached us from them; they might have been dead for aught we knew. I will write no more of this dreadful time, but hurry on to describe the end of our sufferings. As I said, months went by. It was the cruel winter time; the ground was hard with frost, and white with snow. Mother and I were very poor, for no money could reach us from England, and we only lived by the sale of Mother's jewels. M. Jacques still protected us after his rough fashion. Mother would not see him at first after he had denounced Father and Louis, though he said he did so in order to be better able to protect them. But when she fell ill and I did not know where to get money to buy her what was necessary, he it was who suggested to me to sell the jewels, and he it was who disposed of them. He also found us a little lodging near his own, whither we removed as soon as Mother grew a little better, for we could not afford to pay the rent of the old rooms, and besides we were safer in that part of Paris.

I think the day I now recall must have been in December. It was the bleakest, bitterest day of the year. Mother had been ailing all day, and towards evening I slipped out to buy her some white bread. I managed to procure a little and some fresh coffee, and was hurrying home with my prize, finding it difficult to keep on my feet in the fierce wind, when a hand was laid on my shoulder. I started, and looking up saw the not unfriendly face of M. Jacques.

"Did I frighten you, little citizeness?" he said. "Who do you suppose would hurt you?"

"No one, I am sure," I answered hurriedly, "only I am late, and Mother will be wondering where I am."

"My little Toinette desires to see you," he returned; "I came to take you to her."

"Oh, Monsieur Jacques," I said pleadingly, "you know how gladly I will go to Toinette, but let me first attend to my mother; she is ill, she has eaten nothing all day, and I have now been to buy a little coffee and some fresh white bread with which I hope to tempt her."

"My Toinette is ill, too," said M. Jacques, "and she says none can smooth her pillow and sing her songs as you do; you must come, little citizeness."

Evidently he meant to be obeyed; tears filled my eyes, but I only said:

"You must allow me first to tell my mother."

Without waiting for an answer I began to run upstairs; Monsieur Jacques looked after me, "She is a good child," I heard him mutter, then he called out:

"You need not break your little heart by running up those stairs so fast. I will come for you in one hour, and you must be ready."

I thanked him and hurried on till I came to the topmost story, where, waiting first a moment to regain my breath, I opened the rickety door. Our room was only a poor garret with a sloping roof; scantily furnished with a bed, a table, and a few chairs. My mother was lying on a rough couch, which was drawn up by the side of a bright fire—the only luxury we still allowed ourselves. We lived as those around us did, and Mother was no longer known as Madame la Comtesse de Grandville. She had gladly resumed her old name, since the new one, besides bringing back painful memories, had become an added danger. She was thin and worn, but her face grew brighter as the door opened.

"Is that you, Marie?" she said.

"Yes, dearest Mother," I answered; "I'm afraid you think I have been long."

"My darling, it grieves me that you should go out at all in this bitter wind and snow. Come here and take off your cloak, and let me warm your cold hands."

"First, Mother," I said, throwing off my cloak, "we must have some light, and I will show you the beautiful white bread, and make you some coffee, and you will eat and drink to please me."

For a few minutes I busied myself about the room and in preparing the coffee, some of which I brought to her, begging her to drink it for my sake.

"I am better this evening, Marie," said Mother presently, raising herself a little; "you are a good nurse."

"I am so glad," I answered; "because I have to leave you soon for a little while."

"Leave me!" she cried, starting up wildly, "are they going to tear *you* away from me too?"

"Dear Mother, I did not mean to frighten you; it is only Monsieur Jacques who says I must go and see Toinette."

Mother could never hear that name without a shudder, and she said bitterly, "He is our master, you must go of course; it is cruel of him to drag you out again on such a dreadful night."

"Mother dear, it is a very little way, and you know I love poor Toinette; I only grieve to leave you alone."

"My little Marie never thinks of herself," said Mother, making an effort to be cheerful, and stroking my hair; "but do not mind leaving me this evening; I am better, and I must look into accounts; my jewels are nearly all gone now, and if no money reaches us from England our stock will soon be exhausted."

I begged her not to trouble about these things, but to try and get well. Then, fancying that I could hear Monsieur Jacques' step on the stairs, and wishing to save her from the annoyance of seeing him, I kissed her, and throwing on my

cloak again went out hastily, promising to return
as soon as possible.

M. Jacques, with a lantern in his hand, for it
had grown quite dark, was just mounting the
last flight of stairs. He paused when he saw me
ready and wrapped in my cloak.

"Little one, you are early," he said; "I came
to speak to your mother."

"Not tonight, dear Monsieur Jacques," I said.
"She is not well, she could not bear it."

"Not bear it!" he repeated impatiently; "and
what, think you, have we poor to bear every day?"

"Oh! Monsieur Jacques, you forget," I cried,
bursting into tears; "did you not denounce my
father and my brother? Have the poor to bear
seeing those they love torn from them?"

"Only by famine," he said, as he took up his
lantern, and turned to walk downstairs. "If I
denounced your father and brother it was that I
might protect them; it was of them I would speak
to your mother."

"Of them!" I cried, seizing his arm and raising
my eyes to his face. "Oh, Monsieur Jacques, tell
me!"

"Well, little one," he answered, looking down
upon me kindly; "we shall see. Perhaps that will
be best."

We now went on in silence, but the rough man
held my hand tenderly, and suited his pace to
mine. We had not far to go before we reached
M. Jacques' abode. Toinette heard us as we
opened the outer door, and called out eagerly,
though her voice was weak.

"Hast thou been lonely, little one?" said her

father, going to her. "See, I have brought thy friend, the little Marie."

"Thou dear good Father!" she said, putting a wasted arm round his neck as he bent over her; then turning to me she went on: "I have missed thee so, Marie, it is two days since thou hast been here."

"But my mother has been ill; I could not leave her," I answered as I kissed her.

"Well," said M. Jacques, "I can leave thee now and attend to my business, and," he added, turning to me, "I will return in time to take thee home;" then kissing Toinette, and taking up his lantern, he left the room.

Left to ourselves we said little for some time. I was busy attending to Toinette's little comforts, in whose eyes, as they followed me about the room, there was an expression of deep rest and contentment. When at length I took a chair by her side she put out her wasted hand saying:

"Thou hast always seemed like an angel to me, Marie, ever since I opened my eyes and found thee kneeling beside me at the fountain."

"Thou knowest," I answered as I took her thin hand tenderly, "thou knowest that we never forgot thee, though we sought thee in vain."

"That is a long time ago, Marie."

"Nearly two years and a half," I answered sadly.

"And what strange things have happened!"

"Aye, terrible things!"

"But, dearest Marie," said Toinette, "my father says that all the sadness will pass away, and that a time is coming when even you will be happy, when everyone will have enough, and men will live like brothers."

"I do not understand how that can be," I said sighing.

"Marie, thou art sad tonight, thou dost not smile nor sing."

For answer I buried my head in the bedclothes, and burst into passionate sobs. Toinette much distressed soothed me gently, and presently I grew more calm.

"Forgive me, Toinette, I would not distress thee, but I can think of nothing tonight but of my father and my brother; thy father has news of them; it is six months this day since they were taken from us."

"Marie," said Toinette, "I am sure my father will protect them; he has promised me, and you know he has power, the people trust him."

I sighed and said nothing, for though M. Jacques had never lost sight of us since he rescued us from the mob at Versailles, and had helped us often, I feared him more than I trusted him. I could not, however, say this to Toinette, so to avoid the subject I began to sing in a low voice. Christmastime was near, and the words of my song were some learned in my English home, where Christmas was always such a happy time! Oh, how I longed to hear those Christmas chimes again. Tears nearly choked my voice, but I fought them down lest they should distress my poor Toinette. And soon comfort came, as old familiar words reminded me of "peace and good-will among men," and of Him who "rules the raging of the sea, and the madness of the people;"

so I sang on, cheered by these happier thoughts till, looking down, I saw that Toinette had fallen asleep.

A few minutes later Monsieur Jacques came in, and after bending over his daughter for a moment he looked at me strangely, and beckoned me to follow him into the next room.

After he had carefully closed the door he put his hand on my shoulder.

"Little one," he said abruptly, "are your father and brother very dear to you?"

"You know they are, Monsieur Jacques," I answered, as my heart began to beat fast.

"They are in danger," he said; "but I can save them."

"Oh! Monsieur Jacques, and you will, will you not?"

"On one condition."

"Tell me—tell me. I will do anything in the world."

"Look!" said he, "here are two papers; if I write on them the names of your father and brother, they can pass out of the prison free."

"What is the condition?" I cried, as between hope and fear I trembled so that I could hardly stand.

Monsieur Jacques put out his hand to steady me. "Courage!" he said in his rough voice. "You are a brave girl, I believe; now you must prove it. This is my condition. I will provide for the escape of your father, mother, and brother; they shall be taken to the coast, from whence they can cross to England, but you must remain behind."

"I must remain behind! Oh, Monsieur Jacques,

you do not mean it. Have pity! Have pity!" I cried, throwing myself down upon my knees and clasping my hands. "I know you are only proving me," I said faintly; "you mean to be kind, but why did you say such cruel words? I was nearly believing you;" and I looked up into his hard face and tried to smile.

Alas! alas! M. Jacques I believe did not even see me. My anguish—the anguish of my parents —what was that to him? He was seeing only the pinched face of his suffering child. Toinette loved me, and he thought I had become necessary to her happiness.

"I see you are not brave," he said after a moment. "So let it be then! I interest myself no more in your father and brother. They are aristocrats, let them perish with the rest."

In an agony I tried a last appeal.

"Oh, Monsieur Jacques, good Monsieur Jacques, have pity upon us. Think of my mother, who has suffered so much; it will break her heart;" and I began to weep convulsively.

Alas! In my ignorance I had hit upon the worst argument possible. His fierce face darkened, and he put away my pleading hands from his knees.

"Suffered!" he cried, "and has *she* not suffered, my Toinette? Thrown down in her infancy, and left like a common thing to perish in the streets. In want of bread—yes bread, and a stick of wood to light her fire, while you and such as you were decked in silks and satins, and fed to the full; yet we are the workers, while you—you—; but I do wrong to speak of these things to a child," said

Monsieur Jacques, as his eyes fell upon my white frightened face, and he suddenly checked himself. "You are not of them," he went on more softly, "you have been kind to my girl, and she loves you. For your sake I will save your friends. But for yourself, you must make up your mind to remain with me."

Before he had finished speaking I had taken my resolution. Those invisible guardians who watch over children in their weakness surely were at hand to help me in that time of trial, so that fearless and calm I rose to my feet saying, "I have made up my mind; I will remain."

At this moment a faint voice from the inner room called me by name.

"Go to her," said the father; "but remember, not one word of this."

I went and stood once more beside the little bed.

"Art thou still here, my Marie?" said Toinette feebly. "I want thee to kiss me once again. I have had such a beautiful dream; an angel came to carry me to Paradise, and the angel had your face, but he was large and strong, and he had shining wings, and he lifted me up quite easily. I was just floating away when I heard my father's voice, and thine that sounded sad, and that seemed to call me back. Why dost thou weep, Marie?"

"Oh, Toinette," I cried, "ask the angels to take us both, that will be best. Life seems very hard. I am so tired;" and I flung myself down beside Toinette, who threw her wasted arms round my neck weeping in sympathy, while Monsieur Jacques stood looking at us both.

CHAPTER VIII

"FEAR NOTHING EXCEPT DISHONOUR"

How I reached home that night I do not know to this day. I suppose M. Jacques must have half-carried me, for I have a dim recollection of seeing him standing in our little room with his lantern in his hand, and of hearing him tell Mother roughly that I was not well and wanted rest. The next thing I remember is seeing Mother bending over me with a terrified look, chafing my hands. I managed to put my arms round her neck and to whisper to her the wonderful news, telling her at the same time the place of meeting that was appointed for the following night. Mother says that I kept repeating, "Be sure to remember in case I forget, because I am so tired," until I fell into a deep sleep.

When I opened my eyes the next morning it was late, and I saw Mother moving about the room putting together a few little necessaries for the journey. When I tried to move I found my limbs were stiff, and I gladly obeyed her when she told me to lie still.

As for Mother, a new power seemed to have come to her in that dreadful hour, and she who had scarcely moved from the sofa for weeks found strength to nurse and tend me.

I can scarcely recall my feelings during that terrible day. I grudged every hour that went by, and yet I thought that the evening would never come. I remember that wild ideas of escape occurred to me, and then I recollected my promise, and Father's own words came back to me, "Fear nothing except dishonour." Surely, I thought, to break my word now would be dishonour.

When it grew dark, Mother, who was evidently surprised and distressed at my condition, though she asked me no questions, pressed me to eat and drink for her sake. I swallowed something, though I thought every morsel would choke me; then, looking at me all the while with anxious eyes, she helped me to dress, for I could do nothing for myself. When all our little preparations were completed she put out the lights, and we noiselessly prepared to descend the stairs. On the threshold I paused. "Mother," I said, "before we go—in case—in case—we are separated—tell me that I have been a comfort to you." Mother looked at me wildly and drew back. "Marie," she said, "you do not trust M. Jacques. We will not go. My heart misgives me that this is some fresh treachery. What if I were to lose you too?"

These words renewed my courage.

"I saw the paper," I said eagerly. "It is all right; I have no fear. See, I am quite strong and brave now."

Leaning on one another, turning our heads at the slightest sound, we went out into the bitter night. The snow had ceased to fall and the moon was shining brightly. I could not feel the cold, for my head was burning and my heart was beating fast as I thought how much depended on my firmness and courage.

Once we lost our way and almost gave ourselves up for lost, but after wandering for a little time we saw at the top of a long street a carriage stop, and a man get down from the box in whom we recognized M. Jacques. He soon caught sight of us and waved us forward impatiently. At the last moment Mother's strength almost gave way; but M. Jacques came forward, and seizing her arm opened the carriage door and thrust her in. Looking with eager eyes into the carriage I could see her folded in Father's arms, while Louis showered kisses upon her. And then in my ears sounded the dear voice of my father.

"Marie, my child, make haste! Bid Monsieur Jacques farewell; we are waiting for you."

But that stern guardian had his hand on my arm.

"Let me kiss my father once," I pleaded; "then —then I will go with you."

But Monsieur Jacques shook his head.

"Marie, Marie!" cried Mother in an agonized tone, "this delay may ruin all—come!"

Still I only drew further back.

"The child has lost her reason!" cried Mother wildly; and I could see that Father was about to leave the carriage to fetch me, when Monsieur Jacques shut to the door.

"If you leave the carriage," he said, "you forfeit your liberty."

I fell on my knees in the snow praying. He stooped over me and whispered, "I am alone; your father is armed—he can save you if you will."

"My promise!" I gasped, but my voice sounded faraway even in my own ears. I suppose my strength was spent, for I fell forward helplessly.

"It is enough," I heard M. Jacques say in a low voice, and I felt him lift me tenderly and place me in Mother's arms, saying, as they told me afterwards, for I knew no more: "Madame, take your child. I would have kept her—this was the price of the freedom of her parents and brother, but Heaven has willed otherwise. Tell her when she recovers that the angels have taken my Toinette, and that Toinette's broken-hearted father prays evermore for the angel Marie. Adieu! the little one has saved you."

He shut the door, bowing low and removing his red cap of liberty. The carriage drove away. On it went a few leagues, and then the sea—and then—then home!

MARIE FALLS HELPLESSLY AT THE FEET OF
M. JACQUES

CHAPTER IX

SAFE HOME!

AT last the story of those dreadful days is done, and, our troubles safely past, I may tell of our happy homecoming.

We had been long delayed at Dover by my illness, and the soft sun of early spring was shining when once more we drove along the dear old country roads. As we neared the house we could see the budding trees, still leafless, looking almost red against a gray-blue sky, and from the hedgerows the delicate scent of violets and primroses came to us.

Our hearts were beating fast, our eyes were filled with happy tears, as we drove up the village street, and saw our people standing at their doors dressed in holiday attire, and with smiles of welcome on each face. Father, feeling that this was no time for joy, but rather for solemn thanksgiving, had forbidden any ringing of bells or feasting, but the good folk were determined to give us a warm greeting.

On we went, through open gates and up the avenue, till we caught sight of the Yew-tree Walk, and then the garden bright with spring flowers. There was the terrace all unaltered, and at the great door, which was wide open, stood Grandmother, in her lavender taffety with folds of white muslin over her breast, looking out for us and leaning on her stick. By her side stood Nurse, eager and expectant, her very cap-strings quivering with excitement. A little shout went up from the servants who were gathered in the hall, as, with a loud cracking of their whips, the postilions brought us to the door.

In an instant Father had alighted, and without waiting even to help Mother he lifted me in his arms and led me to Grandmother. "Madam," he said, "you must welcome back our little deliverer first."

Then suddenly the servants, led by John the butler, down whose face tears of joy were running, raised a ringing cheer for "Mistress Marie!"

I was so surprised and still so weak from my illness that I burst out crying. I never knew till then that Father thought I had done right, for he and Mother could not bear to speak of the risk I had run.

"Oh, Grandmother!" I sobbed as she kissed and blessed me, "do not let them. I only did what you told me to do. I only tried to be a comfort to Mother."

But dear Grandmother had no time to reply, for Mother came up the steps leading Louis— alas! such a changed Louis, with his golden curls all gone! Nurse seized him for herself, and on all sides were faces bright with smiles of welcome.

Our old home held only happy, thankful hearts that night when we laid ourselves down to rest, safe and secure, under its beloved roof, our strange days in France a memory—nothing more.

CHAPTER X

"GOODBYE TILL WE MEET AGAIN"

A FEW happy months went by. Every day the past became more dream-like to us children, though even I could see that it had left a mark that would never be effaced on Father and Mother. Father never speaks of his own sufferings, which must have been terrible, nor does he even speak harshly of the dreadful French people. I believe he thinks that they had great and fearful wrongs which drove them nearly mad, for once when I was telling him some of the strange things that M. Jacques spoke of to me, he said, "My little Marie, 'to understand everything is to pardon everything.' We must pray God to have mercy on our poor distracted country."

I sometimes fancy I understand a little what my father means, for that dreadful cry for "bread" still rings in my ears. But Mother, who suffered more than any of us, can think of nothing but the wrongs that were committed, and she shudders at the very name of "Liberty."

And Louis, our darling Louis! I shall never forget how changed he was when we saw him the night we escaped, in his coarse clothes, with his hair all matted; and, worst of all, with a vacant look in his blue eyes. How dreadful it is now to see that look return, when something suddenly recalls to him those terrible days! Thank God! this now occurs very seldom, and we all hope that he is beginning to forget.

As I said, a few happy months went by, and then our dear Grandmother was taken from us. She passed away so quietly that it did not seem like death. Up to the very last, though she had grown feeble, and her eyes were dim, she came downstairs and worked at her spinning; but one morning her sight failed altogether, and she pushed her wheel aside, saying with a gentle sigh that her work was done.

Mother comforted her as well as she could, and then we all went to walk on the terrace together, my grandmother leaning on my father's arm. It was a beautiful autumn day, I remember, and the air was still and soft. Grandmother said it brought back to her mind the day when my father had made up his mind to go to France. The thought of all that had passed since then, of the many who had suffered and died, of our martyred King and Queen, saddened us, but Grandmother said to my father:

"My son, take courage, so many noble lives in France have not been lost in vain; the blood of martyrs is accounted as precious seed, remember that; in the end good will triumph, we may be sure."

In the evening we gathered round her again, and sat in silence as the shadows lengthened and day drew peacefully towards its close. She seemed to be dozing, but presently she sat up and took my mother's hand, saying, "Child, you do right to go. Always do your duty."

Mother, who saw that her thoughts were wandering, was frightened, and knelt beside her. Then Grandmother put out her hand, and a most beautiful smile came upon her face.

"Child, child," she said, "do not weep; it is only goodbye till we meet again."

Her arm fell heavily by her side, her head drooped forward a little, and she was gone.

After our dear Grandmother died nothing happened for a long time. My mother grieved bitterly at first, and so did we all; but it was not long before we settled down to our regular life again. My father teaches us himself, and our days are well filled up between work and pleasures.

I am coming now to a great event, and this was how it happened.

There is an old house in the middle of the village which does not belong to my father like the rest, but which was built long ago by a rich draper from a neighbouring town. It is a pretty place, but has been long uninhabited. One day about six months ago what was our surprise to see the doors and shutters of this house open, and workmen busy setting everything to rights. We at once inquired what this meant, and we were told that a fine London madam, a Mrs. Sinclair, was coming to live there with her son and daughter. The village people were of course very curious about these newcomers, and Louis and I were curious too. Some weeks, however, went by before we heard any more about them. At last one Sunday morning, as we were seated in our pew, and the parson was beginning the service, we heard a rustling of silk and the clicking of high-heeled shoes. We cannot see anyone from our big pew in the chancel; but we children looked at one another; we knew these must be the new folk, for no one else in the parish could wear a silk gown. How we longed for just one peep! but there was no chance of that. The service seemed much longer than usual that morning; but at last it was over. We had to wait in our places till everyone was gone, which was, I think, hardest of all; I was so afraid we should miss seeing the new people altogether. Mother, how-ever, did get up a few minutes sooner than usual, and we went out into the churchyard, where the people were all standing about, chatting in the bright sunshine. Mother stopped to speak to some of the old people, but Louis and I ran on to the gate. Just behind our carriage a smart new chaise, with a coachman in canary-coloured livery, was drawn up.

"La! how hot it is!" said a voice behind us; we turned round, and there was this wonderful Mrs. Sinclair, of whom we had thought so much. She was followed by a boy and girl; but at first sight we could think of no one but Mrs. Sinclair her-self. She was tall and big, and I suppose hand-some, but her great black eyes had an expression in them which made me feel uncomfortable. As for her dress it was quite dazzling, the gown of green taffety, very short, showing bright red stockings, and shoes with diamond buckles which sparkled as she walked. Besides all this she wore heavy gold chains round her neck and arms, so I do not wonder that the village folk gaped with astonishment, and thought some real quality had come among them at last.

Louis and I stood aside to let her pass, and then we saw the boy and girl. I scarcely noticed the boy then, though I did just see that he had a coarse red face like his mother's; but the girl! the minute I saw her I loved her. She contrasted strangely with the lady, being plainly dressed in a little brown stuff gown, and she had some shabby covering on her head; but it was her face that won my heart. It was pale, like those sweet lilies that come out in our garden in June; her dark eyes, that brightened when they fell on us, had in them a wistful expression, and her hair was of golden brown that fell in natural wavy curls down her back. Though she was so pretty she seemed to shrink from observation; and, after returning the smile which I could not help giving her, she coloured painfully as if she had done wrong. Still it was not only Edith's beautiful face which attracted me, it was something more. I had a feeling then, and I have it yet, that somewhere, somehow, I have seen her before. Even now, well as I know her, I feel sometimes when I look at her as if I were in a dream from which I shall presently awake, and I often make Louis and Edith laugh by saying that surely I have met her in dreamland.

But I am wandering away from our first meeting. The flies were teasing Mrs. Sinclair's horse, and making him fidgety. The boy noticing this rushed with a loud laugh in front of his mother and pulled a whistle out of his pocket, which he blew close to the animal's ear. The poor thing kicked and plunged, and Mrs. Sinclair, whose foot was on the step of the chaise, screamed and started back, making quite a sensation in our quiet little churchyard. "Oh, Tom!" she cried, "would you kill your mother? What is to be done? What is to be done?"

Taking off his hat, my father now stepped forward. "Madam," he said, "can I give you any help?"

"Oh, sir," she gasped, "you are too good. My poor nerves are so weak—it was but a little jest of my boy's—but I cannot be taken home by that horrid kicking creature."

As she spoke she leaned against the churchyard wall, looking as if she was about to faint. My father hastened to assure her that our carriage was quite at her disposal, and it was soon arranged that we should take her to her own door.

To my mother Mrs. Sinclair poured out apologies for intruding upon us, and Mother, who, though she was dressed only in a simple muslin gown, looked like a princess beside this fine lady, gave her a very distant curtsy. After a little delay, caused by Mrs. Sinclair protesting that she could not get into the carriage first, they both took their seats. The boy Tom, who had been making faces behind his mother's back, was about to jump in next, but my father took him by the arm and held him back.

"You must walk, young sir," he said, giving his hand to Edith to help her in.

Upon this Mrs. Sinclair started up.

"Oh, sir!" she cried, "my darling boy is not strong; he must drive. If there is not room for everyone my niece Edith can walk."

How glad I was even then to hear that Edith was only her niece! Poor Edith shrank back timidly, but my father took her by the hand and almost lifted her in.

"It will do your son no harm to walk, madam," he said. "This little girl has been frightened, and looks tired."

As we drove off, leaving Tom sulking behind, Mrs. Sinclair darted a furious glance at her niece, whose beautiful eyes filled with tears. Oh, how my heart ached at the sight of her sorrow! I could do nothing to help her; I could not even speak a single word of comfort, but I took her hand, and she gave me a loving look, and from that moment we were friends.

My poor friendless Edith! when I think of your sad home, I wonder why my fate should be so different. It is indeed a comfort that I am able to give you some of the happiness out of my life, for we shall always be friends, always—we have promised one another that.

During our first drive we had no opportunity of speaking together, for Mrs. Sinclair talked without ceasing of herself and her affairs. She was delighted with the village folk, whose smiles and curtsies she took to herself, and she spoke warmly of their respect and rustic simplicity.

She told us that, weary of the life of towns, she had come to seek rest and quiet in the country. My mother scarcely spoke, but she looked very kindly at Edith, especially when Mrs. Sinclair praised Louis and me for what she called our comeliness, and alluded slightingly to Edith's pale face and low stature. At the door of the old house where we stopped to put our neighbour down, I was delighted to observe that though my mother hardly touched the aunt's hand in farewell, she leaned forward and kissed Edith.

"My dear," she said very gently, "you must come and see my children. I hope our country air will soon put roses on your cheeks."

"Yes, you must come very often," I whispered; and as poor Edith, who between smiles and tears seemed scarcely to know what to do, tried to thank us, Louis, with his little grand manner that used to make him such a favourite with the French court ladies, handed her out, my father standing back to allow him to do so. Mrs. Sinclair, in the meanwhile, stood in the pretty porch, which was all covered with roses and honeysuckle, looking angry and impatient.

As we drove away I felt that something new had come into my life—a new pleasure and a new pain; for though it was delightful to have found a friend, it grieved me to the heart to think of the sadness of her life. It was, however, pleasant to feel that I might be able to make her happier.

I have heard my father say that the ability to help anyone is a great gift, but that earth can afford no happiness so real as the power to help those whom we love. A beautiful saying, I have always thought, and now I understand it.

CHAPTER XI

EDITH

A FEW days went by, and we saw nothing of our new neighbours, though Louis and I talked and thought of little else. At last, about the middle of the week, as we were sitting at dinner, my father said he thought that since Mrs. Sinclair lived so near to us it would be uncourteous not to call on her.

"But we know nothing of her," said my mother, "and she scarcely seems to be a gentle-woman."

"We know nothing against her," answered my father, "and a visit would only be a civility which need not lead to anything more. Besides, the little niece interested us, and I know Marie is longing for a companion."

"I confess I took a fancy to the child," said my mother; "perhaps for her sake it will be best to be polite to the aunt." Turning to me she added: "Marie, you shall come with me to call this afternoon; it will be a pleasant walk for us."

I coloured with pleasure, for, knowing how

much my mother dislikes such people as Mrs. Sinclair, I had not expected her to be persuaded so easily. Early in the afternoon we started on our visit, and we soon found ourselves at the door of the old house in the village. A black boy, wearing a scarlet coat braided with gold, answered our knock. After looking at us doubtfully, he said "he s'posed we could see missus." Upon this he took us along a passage into a darkened room, where the air was heavy with scent. Here, lying on a sofa, dressed in a faded yellow wrapper, with a turban twisted round her head, was Mrs. Sinclair.

"What do you want?" she screamed out roughly —"another flogging?"

The boy grinned and moved aside, and his mistress catching sight of us jumped to her feet. One angry glance she cast at the boy, then, with the sweetest of smiles, she begged us to be seated. She poured out a thousand apologies for the neglected state of her toilet; she assured us that her nerves were sensitive, that she was a martyr to headaches, and that she was often obliged to spend whole days on the sofa.

My mother, after making a few polite remarks, asked for Edith, whereupon Mrs. Sinclair said peevishly that she believed her niece was out. At this moment we heard through the open window the savage growling of a dog, and a voice in piteous tones saying, "Oh, Tom, pray don't! You frighten me so dreadfully!"

Horrified, I rushed to the window and pushed the blind aside; the scene that I saw at that moment I shall never forget! My dear Edith, looking pale and terrified, was crouching down in a corner made by an angle of the house, and that dreadful Tom was holding with both his hands a fierce ugly bulldog, which he appeared to be setting at her. As I stood trembling with anger and fear he cried out to Edith in his coarse, rude voice:

"You'd better stand still. If you run away my dog will be after you. Now you will have to stay there as long as I choose."

I was so angry that I forgot where I was. Putting aside the blind, I called out:

"You bad, wicked boy, how can you be so cruel?" This so amazed Tom that he let go of the dog, who, hearing a strange voice, began to growl at me; but his master gave him a savage kick, and they both slunk away.

Edith also vanished, and I, remembering where I was, dropped the blind, feeling very much ashamed of my boldness. I looked repentantly at my mother. She shook her head, but I could see she was not really angry.

Mrs. Sinclair had in the meantime thrown herself back on her sofa in an attitude of despair.

"Oh!" she moaned, "that dreadful child Edith! Always in mischief, always irritating my precious boy! What shall I do? It is too much for me; it will be my death."

"Madam," I said eagerly, "indeed it was your son's fault; he was setting his dog at Edith."

"My sweet child," answered Mrs. Sinclair, "you are mistaken, really you are. It was only Tom's fun, nothing more. I grieve to say it, but Edith is sly. I have often punished my poor boy, thinking he had been unkind to his cousin, and afterwards I have found out that she was the one to blame."

I would have spoken again, for I was wild with indignation, but Mother interposed.

"Marie," she said gravely, "you forget yourself. Ask Mrs. Sinclair's permission to go and find her niece in the garden, and I will come for you soon."

"Edith does not deserve the indulgence of Mistress Marie's company," said Mrs. Sinclair, "still, if the sweet child desires to go I will not refuse her. Ah! if heaven had but rewarded me for my goodness to my niece by making her such a child as yours—"

I did not stop to hear more; dropping a curtsy to Mrs. Sinclair, I escaped through a glass door and went in search of Edith. I could not find her in the garden, but upon looking into the orchard beyond I fancied I could see her lying under one of the trees. I passed through a little gate which separates the orchard from the garden and went noiselessly over the grass.

I was not mistaken—it was Edith whom I had seen. Drawing near, but so softly that she could not hear me, I saw that her face was covered with her hands, and that she was weeping. Then I forgot that we were strangers, who had met for the first time only a few days ago. All I knew was, that I loved her, that she was in trouble, and I must comfort her. So the next moment I found myself upon my knees in the long grass, with my arms about her neck. I was crying too—I could not help it. "Edith! Edith!" I said, "I am so sorry."

She drew herself quickly away and jumped up, saying, "Who are you? and what do you want with me?"

"I want to be your friend," I answered; "and I love you already."

A smile shone through her tears as she looked at me.

"I remember you now," she said; "you are the girl I saw on Sunday with a face like an angel. I dreamt of you all one night—the girl that is always happy and always good."

This made me colour and feel confused. "I am happy," I said, "because those about me are good and kind; but—"

"You had much better leave me," interrupted Edith bitterly. "I am not good; I am disagreeable; I have wicked feelings."

"That is not your fault; it is the fault of other people," I said stoutly. "If you had a mother like mine—"

"If—if—" said poor Edith; and then she broke off abruptly. "Your mother kissed me," she went on in a low voice; "kissed me. It made me feel so strange, I could not forget it."

Had no one then ever kissed her in her life, I thought as I listened. I dared not ask the question, but my whole heart went out to her in sympathy. During the short silence that followed her face changed; the sadness that had made it beautiful when she spoke of my mother's kiss departed, and a bitter, angry expression took its place.

"What is the use?" she cried out; "what is the use? Ask my aunt; ask my cousin Tom what I am—they will tell you. They are telling your mother now most likely. She will hear that I am wicked, and ungrateful, and sly; that my aunt gives me everything I have, the very bread I eat; I have heard it so often, and it is true—true; and I hate her. Yes," her eyes gleamed, "I hate them all—I hate the world. When I am grown up, and can do as I like—;" there she stopped, and the strangest expression came into her face. "One cannot run away from the world," she said in a low awed voice.

She looked at me—one would have said that a sudden fear had come to her. I put my arms round her and she did not repel me, she was trembling in every limb.

I begged her in a broken voice to be comforted. "Come to us," I said, "and you will find that the world is not such a dreadful place. I love you, and you shall be my sister, and Louis shall be your brother, and our father and mother—. Edith! Edith! why do you look so strange?"

"Go away!" she said passionately; "go away! Leave me to myself. No one loves me—no one ever will."

I hesitated for a moment; I was almost in despair, but I could not leave her so. Then a new thought came to me quite suddenly, it was just as if an angel's voice had whispered it in my ear.

"Edith," I said very low, "you know we all belong to our Heavenly Father, and perhaps He loves those best who have no one else to love them. Perhaps He sent you here that we might care for you."

We were quite silent for a few minutes. The sun shone, the light wind rustled in the leaves above our heads, and the birds sang their happy songs in the branches, while "one of His little ones" was for the first time casting her burden upon her Lord. It was a moment I can never forget. When I ventured to look again at Edith I saw that her tears had ceased, and that she was smiling.

"It seems too good to be true," she said, "but perhaps it is so; I will believe it because you and your mother do. Marie, I am not worth having for a friend. I am often disagreeable—you will have to be patient with me."

I was so rejoiced at the change in her that I could have jumped with joy.

"Never mind," I said, "I shall not be a bit surprised if you are cross sometimes, because I shall know that you have a great deal to vex you; but Louis will not be impatient with you even if I am. Oh! we shall have such happy days together."

Then we kissed one another and settled ourselves down for a talk under the apple trees. Scarcely had we done so, however, before we saw my mother and Mrs. Sinclair coming through the orchard gate. At sight of her aunt, who beckoned to her impatiently, the colour fled from Edith's face, and the sullen expression, which our talk had chased away, returned. "Never mind her," I whispered, as we went forward hand in hand.

Mrs. Sinclair told her to go to the house at once. "I see," she said, turning a smiling face to me, "that my niece has been in one of her tantrums; I hope you will excuse her."

I suppose my mother saw my face flush, for before I could reply she bade me make my curtsy to Mrs. Sinclair and bid her goodbye. "I hope you will let both the children spend the afternoon with us on Saturday," she said, as she took a very stately farewell of our new neighbour, who, with a profusion of thanks, accepted the invitation for them.

I looked at my mother gratefully, even the prospect of Tom's company could not damp my pleasure in looking forward to having Edith all to ourselves. I counted the hours to the time appointed, and when Saturday dawned fair and bright I could hardly control my impatience.

They were to be with us in time for dinner at noon, and long before then I stood on the terrace steps watching for them.

At last the smart chaise appeared—Tom and Edith were sitting inside; the horse was restive, and no wonder, for Tom had a long whip in his hand, with which he was lashing the poor creature. As they drew up the lash curled round and caught Edith's face; she started up white with pain—a cruel red streak across her cheek. Louis, who had heard the sound of wheels, came out. Though our Louis is only a boy he has the spirit of the finest gentleman in the land. When he saw what had happened the colour sprang to his face, he rushed at Tom and wrenched the

whip from his hand, and in another moment, but
for the interference of our father, who was coming down the steps to welcome our guests, it
would have fallen on Tom's own shoulders. I
confess, for my part, I should not have been
sorry to see the punishment inflicted. He deserved it—he deserved it richly. But I saw at once
that our father was right.

"Louis," he said sternly, "you forget yourself.
Young Mister Sinclair is your guest. The blow
to his cousin was an accident; we must at least
hope so." Then turning to Tom: "Since, however,
sir, you do not understand how to use a whip,
this one shall do no more mischief."

As he spoke he broke the whip in several pieces
and flung them away.

I had in the meantime thrown my arms round
Edith's neck, and was welcoming her to my home.
I found to my sorrow that she was frightened
and ill at ease; even my mother's gentle greeting
brought tears to her eyes, and she scarcely re-
sponded at all to my words and looks of affection.
As for me I was full of indignation against Tom.
It was he who was spoiling our day. Why need
he have come when we none of us wanted him?

After dinner, Louis, who had keenly felt our
father's reproof, and who was anxious to make
amends, proposed that he and Tom should ride
together. At this Tom's sulky face brightened,
and my heart grew lighter, for I had begun to
fear that the day to which I had looked forward
with so much pleasure would end in disappoint-
ment. We watched them start, and afterwards,
as soon as I had my mother's leave, I carried Edith

off to the Yew-tree Walk. There, close to
the old sundial, we found a shady spot, threw
ourselves on the grass, and began to talk.

At first Edith would not speak much. She
wanted, she said, to forget her aunt and Tom,
and to be happy. So I found myself telling her
about things of which I had never spoken much
to anyone; of our beautiful Queen and her sufferings, and of Toinette, whose death set me free,
and whose memory was very dear to me. After
all was it not her gentle influence that saved us.
Edith seemed strangely interested in hearing of
Toinette; her sorrows, she said, touched her more
than those of the Queen and the great people.
After a time she began to speak of her own life.
I found, to my great surprise, that she had never
known her father or her mother. She believes
her mother was Mrs. Sinclair's sister, but even of
this she is not sure, while of her father she knows
absolutely nothing. Once she used to ask Mrs.
Sinclair questions about herself; but she has long
since ceased to do so, for she has been told again
and again that there is nothing to hear, save that
her father's name was Smith, and that she is an
orphan. She does not remember ever having had
any other home than with her aunt, but she
thinks when she was younger she was more
kindly treated. She had a servant of her own
then—an old French nurse—the only creature in
the world, said my poor Edith, who ever loved
her. Once a year a strange old man used to
come to see her aunt, and then she would be
dressed up and shown off; but, child though she
was, she remembers that she used to shrink from

him in terror, and that he seemed to regard her
with dislike.

Some years ago these visits ceased altogether,
and it was then that Mrs. Sinclair became hard
and cruel, and complained bitterly of being bur-
dened with her. After a terrible scene, the old
nurse, who had not been able to bear patiently
the ill-treatment of her darling, was sent off, and
on so short a notice that it was only by stealth
she could bid her nursling farewell. In the
moment of parting she slipped into Edith's hand
a packet containing five gold pieces and a locket,
which she said she had found tied round her
neck when, as a baby, Edith had been placed in
her charge to be taken to England, and which
she had guarded carefully for her. The locket
Edith has worn ever since. She showed it to me;
it is of beaten gold old and worn, with two
hearts entwined, and the letters 'A' and 'I'
engraved on its surface; within are the same
letters traced out in hair of two colours, one
quite black, the other of a golden brown like
Edith's own. "It is my only treasure," said the
poor girl fiercely. "I will never part with it, and
perhaps someday my gold pieces will help me to
freedom." She started up when she said this,
and her eyes flashed.

"Edith," I said, "don't talk like that, things
won't be so bad for you, now you are near us."

"Marie," she cried out bitterly, "you little
know what my life is. I could work—I could
die for anyone I loved, but to be taunted and
despised, to owe the very bread you eat to those
who hate you—"

"Hush, my child," said a gentle voice behind us and my mother laid her hand on Edith's shoulder. "I have not listened to your talk," she said smiling at our confusion, "but I overheard the last words. My dear," to Edith, "you are very young to have so much sorrow."

"Oh! madam," answered Edith, "pray forget what I said. I am not always so."

"I know, my dear child," said Mother softly. "Marie and I have felt trouble. There was a time when we found it very hard not to hate the world."

"You hate!—you!" said Edith very low.

"It was our dear Lord who saved us from the bitterness of hatred," said my mother, her eyes filling with tears. "He will help you if you ask Him. Those who suffer are his brothers and sisters. Will not that assist you to bear?" she asked with a sweet smile.

"It will, it will, and I shall try to be good for your sake and Marie's," said my dear Edith earnestly. Then Mother kissed her tenderly, and we went back to the house together.

Since that day we have often seen Edith. For her sake my father and mother are civil to Mrs. Sinclair, and for her sake Louis endures Tom, who, I think, becomes more and more odious every day. My father has even persuaded Mrs. Sinclair to allow Edith to join us in some of our lessons, and we are constantly together.

Sometimes she looks so bright and happy and is so full of fun; but there comes too often a sad day, when I see a dreadful hunted look in her eyes; and I know then that they have been using her cruelly. She never speaks of what has happened. She told me once, when I reproached her for this, that talking of these things did no good. So long as she lived with her aunt she owed her certain duties, and to speak against her would be disloyal. She says she has learned this since she has been with us; but I know it is the teaching of her own true heart, and we all honour her for her silence.

CHAPTER XII

THE MARSEILLAISE

JANUARY 16th—I have now brought my story down to the present time, and something very pleasant is going to happen.

A few evenings ago, when we were all sitting in the Oak Parlour—Mother and I spinning, and Father reading to us—he put down the book, and sat silent for a few minutes.

Presently he said to my mother: "Today fortnight will be Louis' birthday, and I think we ought to keep it in the good old way."

Mother looked up with surprise. "You do not surely wish it," she said.

"I do," he answered decidedly; "for the children's sake."

"But would not dancing and merriment seem a little out of place to us now?" asked my mother.

"I do not think it should be so," he replied. "We must not forget that we owe something to our neighbours. I am an English gentleman as well as a French Noble, and our children must be trained to the duties of their station."

"Perhaps you are right," said my mother, but she sighed as she spoke.

"Dear wife," he returned, "we must not dwell too much on the sad side of life. The old home has always been famous for hospitality, and our neighbours begin to think us strange and unfriendly. Come, children, fetch me your mother's tablets, we will make a list of the guests, and tomorrow the invitations shall go out for Louis' birthday party."

In the old days, before we went to France, there had always been a gay party to celebrate Louis' birthday, and to this good old custom our father had determined to return. Having made up his mind, he enters with spirit into all the preparations. He will have Louis and me practice our steps for the minuet, and he even takes pleasure in planning our dresses; Louis is to wear a blue velvet coat, with ruffles of fine lace on wristband and shirt front, and I am to be dressed in pink satin. Father says we must both look our best for the credit of "la belle France," as well as of our dear home. My mother seems to dread the day, but Father laughs at her fears and says she will outshine all the other ladies.

January 25th—We can talk of nothing but the great event, and of course it is impossible for me to write of anything else. Today a great and unexpected happiness has come to me. Edith and Tom are coming to our merry-making. It would be no merry-making to me without my dear friend, and her aunt would not let her come unless we asked her cousin with her. I wish Tom no particular harm, but if he could be attacked by a slight illness—a cold, or a disturbance of his nerves, which his mother says are so delicate—before this great day, I do not think I should cry my eyes out. Since they accepted the invitation I had been greatly troubled about my dear Edith's toilet. Her aunt is so unkind, so spiteful. "What," I said to myself, "if she dressed her purposely in some ugly unbecoming way?" And today all my fears have been set at rest. Early in the forenoon my mother called me into her room, and there on the bed were laid out two of the loveliest dresses I have ever seen—each of pink satin exactly alike, and clocked stockings and shoes to match. "They are for Edith and you, my Marie," she said kissing me. My darling mother, this is just like her, to have known what I was thinking of. I can never thank her enough.

January 31st—All is ready, the great hall is cleared for dancing, the garlands are hung, and the musicians are in their places, scraping at their fiddles. Edith is here looking lovely in her pink satin dress, and Louis—our darling, I have no words to tell how he looks—God bless him on his birthday! Father is standing beside Mother in the hall, ready to receive our guests; I hear the first coach coming up the drive, I must go down. How happy I am today!

.   .   .   .

February 3rd—This is the first day I can bear to look at my journal. I have just been with Father; he says I must try to be calm and govern my feelings, or I shall add to Mother's troubles. Perhaps if I write down all that has happened it may help me to collect my thoughts.

Everything went merrily at first on the evening of our ball. Our neighbours came from miles round; old friends of my father, whom he had not met for years, grasped him by the hand, everyone was bright and happy, and the room resounded with music and merry laughter. As for Edith, her face was so radiant and she looked so pretty in her new dress, that all the people were asking me who she was. Tom scowled in a corner, and his mother, who, for all that she was arrayed in gorgeous colours, with bird of Paradise feathers in her head-dress, was taken little notice of, looked affronted and ill at ease. I am sorry to be obliged to confess that it gave me pleasure to see her mortified. I avoided looking at her when I passed by the corner where she sat, and, forgetting that Tom was our guest, I seized one or two occasions for holding him up to ridicule. Ah! why did not all the punishment fall on me?

Before supper Louis and I danced our minuet together, as we had learnt to do at the French court. It is new to the people here, and as our country dances are not nearly so pretty, everyone was pleased with it. A murmur of admiration ran through the room, and when we had finished our dance we were called upon to repeat it. There was a pause then, as the musicians were going to supper.

Louis was flushed and excited, and my mother, who always watches him, was coming towards him to bid him rest, when some chords were roughly struck on the spinet which stood at the further end of the room. In the next instant, before anyone knew what was going to happen, there rang through the startled company the loud notes of a boy's voice, "*Aux armes, citoyens!*"

How I managed to preserve my senses I cannot tell. It was the *Marseillaise*, to whose awful music we had listened so often in the days of terror. As it broke now upon my ear, I seemed to hear the trampling of a great multitude; I seemed to see their frenzied faces. I felt once more with sickening horror how the best and noblest in our unhappy France were being carried out to prison and to death. And if these were my sensations what must they have felt—my father, my mother, Louis, who had suffered so much more than I? Thinking of them, I recovered myself; for a moment I even forgot the outrage that had been offered to us. With senses quickened by pain I looked round. Ah, what a scene! The rude singer had been silenced, but I knew who had thus hurt us. It was Tom—Tom Sinclair. I saw his wicked face, I heard his laugh of triumph. And who was this rushing upon him with uplifted arm? Edith—my Edith! She had seized the bow of a fiddle that lay upon the spinet, crying out, "Coward and bully!" she struck him across the face. I would have run to her, for I was frightened; I did not know what her cousin might do, but the next instant I heard a sound that took from me all power of move-ment, and made my heart stand still. A wild shriek rang through the room. I knew whose voice it was, and for a moment I found it hard to preserve my senses. Was it all a dream then —the music and the lights, and the kind faces of our friends and neighbours? Were we back again in the dark days of terror? So he had cried out—our Louis—when the rough men came to our house and tore him weeping from Mother's arms. Trying hard to keep quiet and to understand things, I looked round. Louis had fallen back fainting; Mother was supporting him; my father, pale with agitation, stood beside them; there were whisperings among our guests, none of whom seemed to know what to do; one or two ladies screamed out that the place was on fire. Mrs. Sinclair was shrieking at the pitch of her voice that she was dying, and imploring those near her to fetch a doctor. Where all had been gay and bright, there was nothing now but confusion and alarm. I am told that all this lasted only for a few moments, though to me it seemed that hours had gone by since our pleasant dance. I must have nearly swooned away myself, when my father's touch and voice revived me. "Marie," he said, "we must rouse ourselves. Come with me."

He led me to the dais at the upper end of the room. "My friends," he said in a loud clear voice, "I beseech you to be calm. By a shocking misadventure some of the terror of the past has intruded upon our joyful present, and the shock has been too great for my son. He and his mother will retire, but my daughter and I bid you to the supper-table."

His words had a tranquillizing effect, but it was impossible to bring back the gladness that had been. Our guests followed us to the supper-table, and we supped in haste as those might do who had a journey before them. Then with many expressions of sympathy they took their leave.

As soon as I could get away I rushed to Louis and Mother. It was a sad, sad night we spent by Louis' bed. If for a moment the vacant expression left his dear blue eyes it was only to give place to one of terror. But at last, as the chill winter dawn began to break, his restlessness passed away; he looked up, recognized our mother and smiled; then over his poor worn face, so changed by these few hours of suffering, there stole a look of peace, and he slept. Very solemnly my dear father knelt, and, with my mother's hand in his, uttered a few words of earnest thanksgiving for the dear life given back to us once more, and soon afterwards I crept away to rest.

How gladly I laid aside the fine clothes I had put on with so much pleasure! I threw myself on the bed, and—forgive me, my darling Edith—in a few minutes I was sound asleep.

We awoke to find a white world. There had been a great snowstorm in the night, and the snow, which had drifted here and there into great heaps, made our garden look changed and unfamiliar. I had slept late, and when I went downstairs I found all our garlands and decorations had disappeared, and everything had fallen into its old place.

My father, who was in the Oak Parlour, said that Louis was better, and that he and my mother would dine with us at noon. It was quite understood among us that when poor Louis' fits passed away no allusion was to be made to them; this was the advice of a famous London physician. I was told that now he remembered nothing after dancing the minuet with me, when he thought he must have fallen asleep, and he was quite perplexed by his extreme weariness. He would not be kept quiet, and to satisfy him, he was to be allowed to dine with us as usual.

Though I found it very hard to conceal my feelings when I saw him—for Louis and I are accustomed to tell each other everything—I managed to say nothing and to look as usual. We sat down to dinner quietly, but almost directly afterwards we heard voices in the hall.

"What can be the matter?" said my mother; "John," to one of the men, "say I cannot see anyone today."

"Possibly," said my father rising, "it is one of our neighbours who has been caught in the snowstorm. I was almost afraid we should hear of some mishap."

As he spoke the door was burst open, and, in spite of the indignant remonstrances of the servants, Mrs. Sinclair thrust herself into the room.

"I insist on seeing Mr. Hamilton," she cried; "I will not be denied. If he is harbouring that wretched girl, and refuses to give her up, I will have recourse to the law. I am her guardian; she shall not defy me."

"Madam," said my father sternly, "I am willing to see you, and to hear what you have to say, but not in the presence of my wife and children."

He offered her his arm to lead her from the room, but she dashed it away, pouring out a torrent of angry words. We gathered from what she said, that, when she returned home, there had been a terrible scene between her and Edith, whom she ordered at last to her room to remain there during her pleasure. The next morning it was found that Edith was not in her room, and that her bed had not been slept in. A search was made in the house and garden, but it was in vain, and Mrs. Sinclair had come to us in the belief that if she was not here she had fulfilled her threat of running away. Here the unhappy woman burst into floods of excited tears, declaring that it was an evil day for her when she nourished such a serpent in her bosom.

Oh, how bitterly I reproached myself for having forgotten Edith in the excitement and anxiety of the last night. I have been false to my friend, I said to myself, for should even my trouble about Louis have made me forgetful of one who had only me to care for her.

I glanced at my father; his eyes were fixed on the wide waste of snow, and I had never seen him look so stern.

"Madam," he said, when Mrs. Sinclair ceased, "the poor child is not here. If she has wandered away and is lost among the snowdrifts you are answerable for her life before God, if not before man."

Upon this Mrs. Sinclair burst into a wild fit of weeping. I ventured to touch my father's hand.

"Father," I whispered, "can nothing be done?"

"Something must be done at once," he answered; "perhaps it is not too late to save her; we must send out in all directions."

He began to give some orders to the servants, and my mother went off in haste to prepare for her reception should she be found, while I, remembering suddenly that Mrs. Sinclair had spoken in her ravings of what had happened on that dreadful evening, turned to look for Louis—he was gone. A wild fear seized me, and I flew to seek him, but he was not to be found. I dared not tell my mother. I went in search of my father, whom I found standing in the hall, after having just succeeded in getting Mrs. Sinclair to leave the house.

"Father," I said, "I cannot find Louis."

I think my fear came to him, for when he had heard what I had to say he went out without a word, and as I could not rest, I flung on a cloak and hood and followed him. My father was hastening to the stables, which are some way from the house; the path was almost blocked by snow, but I kept him in view, though I stumbled many times, and plunged into the drifts up to my waist more than once. We reached the yard gate almost together; he opened the door of the stables, and made straight for the stall where Louis' pony was accustomed to stand—it was empty. The men were away at their dinner, so he must have put on the saddle with his own hands, and all down the yard were the marks of the pony's hoofs, now, alas! becoming rapidly effaced, for snow was again beginning to fall. My father took all this in at a glance, and for a moment he hid his face in his hands, then he looked up and saw me.

"Marie, child," he said, "be brave. It is you who must tell your mother; I must go in search of him. Thank God he has not had time to go far."

I think the feeling that I was allowed to share Father's burden helped to give me strength. I struggled back to the house, managed to change my wet clothes, and then I sought out Mother and told her—told her that her darling with his fragile uncertain life had gone out alone in the bitter weather in search of Edith, for I knew that was his errand.

How she bore it I do not know, but I suppose strength does come in our sorest need, for she was calm. We watched together through that terrible afternoon. The darkness gathered; the wind rose, whirling the snow hither and thither, shaking the windows, making wild unearthly sounds, and hand in hand we sat in silence, for we could not trust ourselves to speak.

At length, just as the hall clock struck eleven, we heard the sound of voices. We ran to the door, and saw at once through the darkness the flashing of lanterns, which told us that those we had sent out were returning. How slowly they moved along! and they seemed to be bearing something; was it our Louis, or only—? My heart beat wildly, I felt afraid to move, and yet I longed to run away and hide myself from what might be coming. As for Mother, her courage rose; I think that for her the torture was over when the time for action came.

She drew me with her into the hall—I who should have supported her. All our men had joined the search party, but the women were gathered there, many of them weeping, all excited. "Is everything ready?" asked my mother in her clear calm voice, and then she gave a few orders which were eagerly obeyed.

The steps came nearer, the great oak door was pushed open; my father entered first, went up to my mother and took her hand.

"Courage, dear wife," he said, "our boy is alive; with God's help we shall save him."

As he spoke the men brought in our darling, and laid him in front of the fire. Every effort was made to restore him, but for some time it was in vain. He did not speak, he did not stir; we only knew he was alive by the faint beating of his heart. I was beginning to despair, when at last, after what seemed to me an age of suspense and misery, he sighed, opened his eyes, and looked round him.

"Has Edith been found?" he murmured.

My mother and I glanced at each other in alarm. How were we to answer him? but my father said gently, "Edith is in safe hands."

Louis seemed satisfied with the answer. "I think somehow it was for my sake," he said feebly; "perhaps I shall remember in the morning," and then his eyes closed again, and he slept.

That night as we kept our second watch beside Louis—a hopeful watch this time—my father told us how he had found him some miles away on the London Road. He had lost the track, and had wandered among the snowdrifts, and, overcome by drowsiness, no doubt, he had fallen from his pony. They were both found half buried in snow; the faithful animal had crept close to his master, and it was his warmth probably that prevented our Louis' sleep from becoming the sleep of death.

"And poor Edith?" said my mother. It was a

question I had been longing yet dreading to ask.
Alas! my father shook his head.

"We can find no trace of her," he said; "but
the search is still going on. I think from Mrs.
Sinclair's story that she must have started some
hours before the snow began; in such case she
may have taken refuge in a cottage, and if so
we shall discover her safe and sound when the
weather clears."

He spoke cheerfully, but I felt sure that he
was uneasy, and, my courage giving way, I burst
into tears.

Most tenderly my father soothed and comforted
me. He was determined, he said, after all he had
seen and heard, not to permit Edith, when she
was found, to return to her aunt, but to offer her,
for a time at least, a home with us. He spoke
sternly, almost as if he were angry with himself
for not having rescued her sooner. When I grew
calm I knelt by Mother's knee, and he led our
thoughts to One whose care is ever over us,
without whom "not a sparrow falls to the ground."
To Him we commended all we loved, and afterwards, Mother, saying I was overwrought, put me
to bed herself as if I were a tiny child again, and
I slept.

The next day the snow had ceased, and there
was a hard frost. Nothing more had been heard
of Edith, and seeing that the roads were impass-
able, in some places even dangerous, on account
of the depth to which the snow had drifted,
further search was useless.

Louis remained very drowsy all that day. Towards evening he became feverish, and his mind

wandered; some vague remembrance of the scene at the party seemed to haunt him, for he kept repeating, "I must find her; she was angry for my sake." Whenever he dropped asleep he would rouse himself, and urge on his pony saying, "I must not rest till she is found." The next day he seemed no better, so in spite of the weather we managed to fetch a doctor. He says there is very little to be done, that Louis has had a shock, both mental and physical, and nothing but time and quiet can restore him.

February 4th—The frost continues. Still no news of Edith. Sometimes I think she is dead, that the white snow is her shroud, and that I shall see her no more. But surely—surely—if she were with the happy angels, one could come to let me know that she was at rest! Then I could bear to look into poor Louis' eager eyes, and to tell him that all is well.

But no; I will be brave and patient; I cannot put the dreadful pain out of my heart, but I will press it down; I will help Mother and Father, and cheer my darling brother, and perhaps—someday—God will give my friend back to me.

CHAPTER XIII

A STRANGE MEETING

MARCH 25th—The weeks have gone by sadly since I last opened my journal; I have had no heart to write, and now spring is at hand. How unlike other springs it seems, when the soft air has been warm with sunshine, and alive with singing birds! All is cold and dreary, the trees stand brown and bare, with no sign of swelling buds; primroses are still buried in their winter sleep, and even the sweet violets come out slowly and unwillingly. Folks say that the great snowstorm and the frost that followed it will make this year remembered for many generations. We at least shall not forget it. For my own part, I feel that life will never again appear the same. I do not want to be self-ish and repining; every night I try to thank God as I should for all the blessings He has given me; but my heart will never stop aching till I know Edith's fate.

When the roads became passable, my father made every effort to trace her. He had all the villages in our neighbourhood searched; and he inquired of the people belonging to the stage-coaches whether anyone answering to her description had been observed to take a place; but if that was the way she went, either the time was too long gone by for any to remember, or they had been occupied too much with their own concerns to have taken notice of her, for we have not obtained the slightest clue to help us in our search.

Father, I think, begins to fear that she perished in the snow; I still cling to hope. But should I call it hope? Ought I to be comforted by hoping that she is alive—alone and friendless in a world that can be so cruel to the poor? Thus I ask myself at times, and then feel that I could have borne it better if we had found her stiff and cold under the snow, and laid her in the quiet church-yard; for then I should have known that loving angels had carried her away, that she was safe from sorrow forever. If I could but believe, Mother says, that, wherever she is, a Love far more mighty than mine is about her, I should feel less sad. I must pray for more faith and patience.

This is not our only trouble. Louis has never quite recovered the events of that dreadful night; though he gets up and about as usual, he is often weary now, and the least exertion seems to be too much for him.

He remembers his journey through the snow to look for Edith, and he often speaks of her; but it is always as of one dead. He cherishes her memory most lovingly, and says she suffered for him. We do not know exactly what he means by this, and we never ask him, but pass away from the subject as quickly as possible, as we dread exciting him.

As soon as the frost broke up, Mrs. Sinclair and Tom disappeared from the village. We never saw either of them after the day of the storm, but we heard that Mrs. Sinclair took great pains to conceal where they were going when they left. So the old house in the village is empty again; but that is well, as we do not want any new neighbours.

March 27th—Today the east wind, which has been blowing steadily for a long time, left us, and the air became soft and balmy. After dinner Father told me to get ready to walk with him. He talked as we went along, telling me of his anxiety about Louis—an anxiety even deeper than that of our mother, who cannot see that her darling is failing. He said, too, that he was grieved to see my face looking sad and changed.

"Oh, Father," I began, "I am so sorry—"

"I do not blame you, Marie," he said; "trouble is very hard to bear at your age, when life appears endless, and when the possibility of forgetting seems a treachery."

How exactly my father reads my thoughts! I took his hand, for I could not speak, and he smiled and went on:

"But sometimes, my Marie, when remembering does no good to those we love, and unfits us for the duties of life, it is right and wise to forget— as far as we can," he added, reading the protest in my face. He then went on to say that he had determined to see what a change would do for us all, and that, with Mother's consent, he had taken a house in London for two months, whither we should set out on our journey next week.

This was a great surprise to me, and regret mingled in my feelings. I think every day that Edith may walk in, for surely she will come to us when her five gold pieces are spent—and if she were to come and find us gone! But then I remembered our faithful servants, who will be sure to care for her. I will tell them to be ready, so that whether she comes by day or night, she will know that she has been expected.

When this was settled, I will confess that the prospect of a change became pleasant to me. London is a wonderful place. Who knows what the great physicians there may do for Louis? and there are other things;—but I must not spend my time in dreaming. A week is a short time in which to prepare for such a journey, and I must try to help Mother, who will have much on her mind.

April 2nd—Our trunks are packed, and everything is ready for our start. We go tomorrow, leaving home early, so that we may arrive in good time at the end of our first day's journey. Louis has looked very bright and happy the last few days, which has pleased us all, and I have been busy and cheerful. Am I already beginning to forget? I do not think so. The memory of Edith is with me always.

I promised Mother to go to bed early, so I must not write more. When I next open my journal we shall be in London.

April 10th–Queen's Square, London. We have arrived here in safety, after passing three days and nights on the road; our journey was not unpleasant, though a little fatiguing, especially to Mother and Louis, and we were not molested, which, as the roads have lately been infested with highwaymen, was no small mercy.

The house our father has taken for us is in a quiet square; we hear in the distance the din of voices, and the tread of many feet, but from our windows we can see green trees where birds build their nests. Sometimes we only know we are in town by the loud rapping at our neighbours' doors, as ladies in their sedan chairs go to pay visits at the fashionable hour.

My chief pleasures as yet have been walking through the streets, and watching the people as they hurry by, all full of business. I delight also to be in the crowded city, and to see the broad river, where great vessels, laden with strange things from all parts of the world, come and go; I think I shall never tire of these wonderful sights.

*April 15th–*We have quite settled down to our new life, and already some comfort has come to us. Two famous physicians have seen Louis; they both agree that he is suffering from no active disease, and they promise that time and care will restore him. As yet he does not seem much better, but Mother says that she can see an improvement, and that Father and I are too impatient.

We have fallen into our old ways, for Mother is far too much occupied with Louis to care for entering into society; she says, besides, that the society of town, card-parties, and gossiping would not please her, so we live as quietly as if we were at home. Sometimes old friends, whom Father and Mother knew years ago, come to see us, and take a dish of tea with us; but for this we see no one.

In the morning I read with Father, and in the afternoon he takes me out with him, while Mother and Louis drive to the parks, or to the village of Islington, which is close by, where there are fair fields and green lanes to refresh country eyes.

April 20th—A very strange thing has happened to me. Yesterday afternoon my father took me with him to the city, whither some business called him. He was set down in one of the most crowded streets, and I, remaining in the coach, found amusement, as I always do when I am alone, in watching the passers-by. After a time I noticed an odd-looking man, who passed and repassed the coach, peering inside curiously. He was very poorly dressed, and his hat was drawn down over his face so that it was hardly possible to distinguish his features. Feeling interested, but half-frightened, I leaned forward to see him better; and he, moved as it seemed by a sudden impulse, raised his hat and bowed. A moment later and he had disappeared.

Perplexed and disturbed I sat dreaming in my place. A thousand memories had awakened in my mind as the years rolled back; once more the Paris mob was surging around us; once more I heard the clash of their murderous weapons, and the awful, never-to-be-forgotten cry, "*A la lanterne–les maudits à la lanterne!"*

I closed my eyes to shut out the dreadful scene, and when I awoke from my dream I knew that it was the face of M. Jacques that I had seen. With a great effort I controlled myself, for I knew that if my father saw my agitation he would take me home, and perhaps never let me come out with him again; so when, after some little time, he returned, I was able to tell him calmly whom I believed I had seen. He said I was nervous and fanciful, but I still maintain that I am right. This strange M. Jacques may have been sometimes harsh and cruel to us, but I believe he meant kindly. He certainly saved our lives more than once. I think I should like to see him again; and how pleasant it would be to do something to help him for Toinette's sake! This is the thought that has been haunting me.

April 24th–I was right. I went out today with my father; we stopped where we did before, and again the same man appeared. He passed backwards and forwards twice, slowly and feebly. Each time I saw him I felt more convinced that I had not been mistaken. At last I summoned up all my courage, put my head out of the coach window, and called out, "M. Jacques!" At the sound of my voice he stood quite still and appeared uncertain what he should do; then he turned round and uncovered his head. It was indeed M. Jacques, but how changed!–his hair gray, his eyes dull and sunken; his figure, that had been so erect, bent and shrunken. The sad change made all my fear vanish away. I felt now only an intense pity for his sorrows, and a great desire to help and comfort him; for now that Toinette was dead I knew that he had no one in the wide world to care for him.

"Will you come and speak to me?" I said in French. "Do you remember me?"

"Remember you, little mademoiselle!" he answered, coming close up to the coach, still holding his hat in his hand; "shall I ever forget you? The wonder is that you deign to remember me; but the angels never forget!"

As he spoke of the angels I know his thoughts flew to Toinette, for tears filled his eyes.

"Oh!" I cried, not knowing what to say, "I am so sorry for you, M. Jacques! Are you all alone here? Can we not help you?"

There was something of the old proud ring in his voice as he answered me:

"I did not approach mademoiselle to ask favours," he said, "only"—his voice grew softer —"to look again on her sweet face, to kiss her hand, to ask her pardon, and to bid her adieu forever."

At this moment my father appeared, and it would be difficult to describe his astonishment.

"Father," I cried, "this is M. Jacques!"

For a moment these two stood confronting each other. I can guess what each was feeling—my father, the gentleman, justly proud of his high name and stainless life; and the stern republican —the man who, for the sake of his ideas, had trampled on what we hold most sacred, who had even, it might be, helped to shed innocent blood. My heart beat high as I watched them. Was there anything that could bring them together? Yes, there was one thing. My father was of too noble a nature not to acknowledge a favour, most of all when it came from an enemy, and he it was who made the first advance.

"I am glad to meet you," he said, holding out his hand. "I owe my life and the lives of those I love to you. If we in our turn can help you—"

M. Jacques did not suffer him to finish. Thrusting aside the offered hand, he said: "You owe me no thanks, monsieur; thank—"

But here his voice grew faint, he became deadly pale, and would have fallen had not my father caught him. A crowd began to gather immediately, and Father hastily ordered that he should be placed in our coach. This having been done, we drove off quickly to the nearest doctor. When we arrived M. Jacques was still insensible; he had to be carried into the house, and my father anxiously inquired what was the matter.

"The matter!" was the reply; "starvation! You are shocked? Well, it is bad; but we get used to it. These poor foreigners come over thinking to find our streets paved with gold; they find instead death from want too often. Give him plenty of brandy now, and a good meal afterwards; that will set him up till he gets hungry again."

So saying the doctor took his fee, and left us in his waiting-room in the greatest perplexity. M. Jacques' head lay on my lap, and I was trying to get the brandy down his throat.

"This is no fit work for you, Marie," said my

father uneasily, "but I scarcely know what to do."

"Father," I said, "do let us take him home to
be nursed. There is an unused room at the top
of the house."

"But your mother!" objected my father. "You
know she always mistrusted this man, and to
have him suddenly brought into the house might
be too great a shock for her; besides, there is the
risk of Louis recognizing him."

"There is no necessity for Louis to see him," I
urged; "and you need only tell Mother that we
found him dying of starvation, and that we have
brought him home for charity. I do not think
she will remember him; no one knew him so well
as I did."

My father thought for a minute, then he called
up the coach, had M. Jacques once more placed
inside, gave the order, "Home as quickly as possible;" and at present our strange visitor is lying
in an upper chamber of this house. He is sen-
sible, but as weak as a little child and unable to
speak. Mother took his coming without surprise,
being too much concerned about his sufferings to
feel any curiosity as to how we found him. She
goes in and out of his room tending him, and the
servants take it in turns to watch beside him.

April 28th—M. Jacques is still here. After he
had been with us two days my father began to
be uneasy about Mother, fearing it would shock
her to hear the name of her guest; but while he
was wondering how he should tell her, M. Jacques
unconsciously took the matter into his own
hands. One morning when Mother was standing
beside him feeding him, for he can do nothing

for himself, he said feebly:

"Madame, do you know whom you are suc-couring?"

Mother looked at him carefully; she turned a little paler, and said gently:

"Someone in sore distress; I know no more —that is quite enough."

"What, madame!" he exclaimed, "have they not told you that I am M. Jacques—the man who would have robbed you of your child? for I would have kept her because my little one loved her. Alas! the good God punished me by taking away my Toinette."

I could see that, as he spoke, a sore conflict was going on in Mother's heart. The past was un-folding itself before her, and she had to struggle with a feeling of aversion. But after a few mo-ments her kind nature triumphed, and she said gently:

"I thought I remembered your face. Be calm. I cannot have you distress yourself so. You did not rob me of Marie, and you restored my dear ones to me. I think the good God has sent you to us in your trouble, and we are glad to be able to help you."

"Say one word—pardon," he prayed.

Again there was silence for a while, then Mother took his hand, and said very solemnly, "If there is aught to forgive, I forgive with all my heart."

The sick man closed his eyes, utterly exhausted; Mother did not leave him till he fell asleep; then she beckoned to me to follow her, and we went to my father.

"Husband," she said, going up to him and taking him by the hand. "Did you doubt me? Whoever this man is, do we not owe him life itself?"

Father knew directly what she meant.

"Dear wife," he answered, "do I doubt that your every thought is better and wiser than mine? I was silent because I feared the dreadful memories his name would bring before you; and your life is so frail—so frail and so precious!"

I did not wait to hear more. I crept out of the room, my heart too full for words; but on my knees I asked God to make me worthy of such parents.

May Day—The streets are gay with the poor sweeps making holiday, and in all the villages round about London the May-pole is set up; there is plenty of junketing and merry-making everywhere.

M. Jacques has recovered enough to be able to sit up every day; he is silent, but very grateful, only he begs us to let him leave us, which, however, Father and Mother will not hear of his doing yet. Louis continues much the same; he has seen our strange guest; but happily he does not remember him at all, nor does he connect the name with anything in the past, of which he has really but a dim recollection when he is in a natural state of mind.

May 10th—My father goes upstairs every day, and has long talks with M. Jacques, who has told us much of his history. It is an interesting story, though very sad. I happened one day to say that I should like to have it written down in my journal. M. Jacques seemed touched at this desire on my part, and anxious to gratify me. Though his knowledge of English is quite sufficient to enable him to carry on a conversation with ease, he would find it difficult to express himself accurately in writing, so we have arranged that he is to dictate his story to me in French, and I am to write it down in English, as nearly as possible word for word.

My dear father often converses with me in French, so that the two languages are almost equally familiar to me.

How little I thought, when I began to write in my book only a few short months ago, what wonderful events would be recorded in its pages!

CHAPTER XIV

MONSIEUR JACQUES' STORY

THE little Mademoiselle Marie has asked me to tell my story for her to write in a book which she calls her journal. It seems strange that my dark sad story should be written on the white pages of mademoiselle's book—white like the pure soul the good God has given her; but she wishes it, and what would I not do to obey the desires of the angel who has more than once beckoned me from destruction? Shall I begin at the end, and tell how, when life was nearly over for me, I saw her sweet face again? how her gentle voice called me, and, as in a dream, I obeyed? how my brain reeled, and I knew no more, until I found myself—I, the outcast—nobly rescued and tenderly succoured?

Ah! my little lady, I would not that you should dwell on that in these fair pages; my mind shall travel back rather to scenes that seem to me now like those of another life—to the days when I too

was young, and when I saw the future lying before me all golden in the distance. If, as my
story goes on, and I tell how this golden future
turned to blackest night, my heart grows fierce
with a bitterness which I cannot always control;
if I make your blue English eyes grow dim with
tears for wrongs that could not have been wrought
in your free country, you must forgive me, for
the fault is not all mine.

My father was a small farmer, living at the
time when I was born in a little village that lay
among the sunny plains which surround Avignon.
He rented his farm from the Marquis de la Fontenaye, a great Noble, whose château, which he
rarely visited, stood over above our village. It
was a great and stately abode, and we never
spoke of it, or of aught that happened within its
walls, save with awe and reverence. There was
one living there, however, whom no one feared,
and that was the little daughter of the stern
Marquis. Her English mother had died, broken-
hearted, it was whispered, when she was born.
The Marquis came from Paris, where he spent
most of his life, and gave orders that a nurse
should be found for his child amongst the villagers.
It happened that my mother had lost a little baby
born a few days before the daughter of the
château. The messengers of the Marquis came
to her, and she took the little Antoinette, and
reared her as her own.

My first recollections are of long days spent
with my foster-sister wandering through the
woods and vineyards, or resting from the noon-
day heat and eating our simple food in shady

spots by the river. I remember too, how, when
the sun went down, we would go home hand in
hand, and how my mother's goodnight kiss would
be given to us both alike, as we laid our happy
little heads on our coarse pillows. My father,
who was better educated than those about him,
began to teach us when we grew older. He set
us little sums on our slates, which we worked out
together, and made us write and read every day.
He would also tell us wonderful tales—all of
which, he said, were found in books, and formed
part of the history of our country. For me these
stories had the deepest interest. I would listen
to them, watching my father's face, till my mother
would cry out to him to stop. What was the use,
she would say, of learning to such as me? It
could never do me any good; a peasant I had
been born, and a peasant I must remain to the
end of my days. I remember the feeling of re-
sentment that my mother's words aroused in my
heart, and how my father would sit stern and
silent. But sometimes the little Antoinette would
twine her arms round his neck, and say that if I
was a peasant might she not be a peasant too?
and then we would all laugh together, and the
shadow of the future would cease to trouble us.

Many happy peaceful years went by after this
fashion. At last M. le Marquis deigned to remember that he had a daughter, and to inquire
after her welfare. Hearing that she was still in
our humble home, he ordered that she should be
removed to the château. That was a bitter day
for us, but our grief was short-lived. Our little
lady's new attendants, while they provided her

with better clothes and food than she had been accustomed to with us, were careless about the way in which she spent her time, and did not seek to control her. She fell, therefore, very soon into her old ways, spending all her days with my mother. I was obliged now to help my father on the farm; but the work was light, and I was able to devote many hours to Antoinette's society. So again the pleasant years went by.

I was seventeen years of age when the events of which I am about to speak took place. Thanks to my simple bringing up, and the open-air life which I led, I was strong and active; tall, with the limbs of a young giant, they said in the village; healthy and hearty, able to fight, aye, and to suffer, if need were, for those I loved. Our Antoinette, who was in her fifteenth year, was as different as could be from me. She was tall in stature, slender and graceful; her eyes were brown; her mouth was the sweetest that can be imagined, and her hair was of that beautiful golden brown which seems to belong to the women of your race. Need I say that to me she appeared the fairest thing under the sun? My little mademoiselle, you will see that I am lingering, that my tongue halts in its tale; it is that the memory of a day of which I must now write comes over me; the first burning sense of wrong which then filled my heart returns, and I find it difficult to think or speak without bitterness. But for your sake, Mademoiselle Marie, I will be calm.

It was high noon on a lovely day in June. I seem to see, as I write, the deep blue sky overhead; the scent of blossoming limes comes towards

me, and I feel the balmy air. There was nothing
particular to do on the farm, and Antoinette and
I had taken our brown bread and fresh milk out
of doors, and were enjoying our simple meal by
a brook that ran through the woods close to the
château. I had just been reading, I remember,
a book of adventures; and as we sat together I
told her some of the stories it contained. I spoke
also of my longing to go out into the world to see
its wonders.

Antoinette did not agree with me. The life
we led was, she said, perfect. We had the
birds, and trees, and flowers, and sunshine, and
what did we want besides? As for the beautiful sights to be seen in the world, could we see
anything more beautiful than that? and she
pointed to where the woodlands opened out,
showing the broad, beautiful plains of our fair
land, and vine-clad hills in the blue distance. I
raised my eyes, and at that moment a shadow
crossed our path. Ah! cruel shadow, that was to
rest upon us evermore! A gentleman stood before us. He was evidently a great seigneur, for
he bore himself proudly, seeming almost to disdain
the ground he trod on; and beneath the cloak
which was thrown round him we could see soft
lace ruffles and silken hose. For a few moments
he stood looking at us silently, with smiling
mouth, but cold stern eyes. How clumsy I felt,
how awkward and uncouth—I, the peasant's son
—in presence of this fine gentleman! He did not
even look at me as I stumbled to my feet; I
might have been an inanimate thing, a clod of
earth—one of the cattle on his estate would have

claimed more of his notice than I. His eyes were fixed upon Antoinette, who had turned very pale.

"Mademoiselle de la Fontenaye, I presume," he said at length, and there was an indescribable ring of pride in his voice as he spoke the name.

At these words Antoinette rose to her feet and stood before him calmly. Addressing him as Father, she begged his pardon for not having been at home to greet him. Had she known that the honour of his visit was expected, she would have been within doors.

The Marquis smiled, and looked at her with a little more satisfaction. He said at the same time that it was his pleasure to come and go without being expected; then he bade her return to the house with him, and make ready to start for Paris immediately. He was about to lead her away, when she turned to me, and, taking my arm, drew me forward. I was her brother, she said; to me and to her foster-parents she owed everything. Her father must permit her to bid us farewell.

My blood boiled beneath the glance which M. le Marquis, who seemed for the first time aware of my presence, cast on me. So he might have looked on some curious insect that had crossed his path in the forest.

"Ah!" he said slowly. "I remember. It was to the care of these good people that I entrusted you when you were an infant. You are right to feel grateful towards them. Young man"—addressing me; every word of that speech is imprinted on my brain—"pray tell your good parents that Mdlle. de la Fontenaye thanks them for their services, which will not be forgotten by her family. For yourself"—he paused and took a pinch of snuff from a box of gold and enamel —"a well-grown youth," he said under his breath; then aloud, "If you care to follow us to Paris, I will either take you into my own service, or recommend you to the notice of one of the Noblemen about the court."

Three times did Antoinette try to interrupt this speech. As for me, I turned white with rage; for a few moments my anger took from me the power of speech.

"I see," said the Marquis, misinterpreting my silence, "you are taken by surprise. Most natural. Go home, my good youth, and consult your parents. You shall hear from us again."

One tearful glance our Antoinette cast upon me; it was with her as it was with me—speech was impossible. Then, her father beckoning to her impatiently, she turned away.

I watched her white gown disappear in the distance, and when there was nothing more of her to be seen, threw myself on the ground in an agony of sorrow and rage. For the first time in my simple life I realized what it meant in my country to belong to the people. Before me, young, full of energy, possessed, as I then believed, of talent, there was, and would always be, a barrier which I could not cross.

I must not tell you, little mademoiselle, all the bitter thoughts that filled my mind as I lay there in the solitude, my face buried in my hands.

Hours must have passed, for when I looked up the setting sun was reddening the tops of the trees and touching with a golden light the hills in the distance to which Antoinette had pointed. Beautiful and peaceful as was the view, it brought no balm to my wounded heart. I was bitter as well as sorrowful, and the calm loveliness of these familiar scenes did but stir me to a fierce anger against the world. So things, I thought, had always been, so they would be to the end. I might beat my breast against my prison door, I could not burst it open; with all my efforts I should but hurt myself.

I rose slowly, and though I dreaded returning I took my way home.

I found my mother weeping and my father stern and silent. While I was away there had come a messenger from the château bringing a note from Antoinette. My mother showed it to me: it was the letter of a child, hastily written, and blotted with tears. She was going to Paris at once, she said; her father would place her in a convent, where she was to finish her education; he forbade her coming to bid us farewell. Would we remember her always, as she would remember us?

Shortly after the arrival of this note the steward of M. le Marquis came riding up to our door. He brought with him the ceremonious thanks of M. de la Fontenaye, a renewal of his offer to place me out in service in Paris, and a bag containing a hundred louis d'or. The gold my father returned, and with it a message as proud as that which the Marquis had sent to him. He said, moreover, that no son of his should be a valet —even to the King himself. After that he sat silent, and there was on his face the stern, set expression which I knew so well. And indeed we were all sad; with our little Antoinette the joy seemed to have gone out of our house. Only my mother, who had the noble patience of the people, tried to console us. It was right, she said, that our darling should leave us; she had been forgotten too long. We should remember that she belonged to one of the great families of France, while we were only peasants. The next day my mother went about her work as usual, but it was long before the stern look left my father's face, and I do not think he was ever quite the same again. My outward life in the meantime went on as usual. I helped my father on the farm, and spent all my spare hours over pencil and paper, for I believed I had a talent for designing; but I did not delight in it now as once I had done. The loss of Antoinette, and the stony glance of the Marquis, had killed my boyish dreams.

After this fashion a year passed by. My father, though he said nothing, must have noticed the change in me, for, to my great surprise, he told me one day that, having observed my talent for drawing, he had arranged to place me with a famous designer at Lyons. This prospect did not delight me as it would once have done, but I tried to show some pleasure to my father, thanking him, and promising him to make good use of my opportunities. A few days later I left my home for the first time.

The man with whom my father had placed me was a designer of patterns for the beautiful manufactures that have made Lyons famous. He was struck with my facility, and took pleasure in giving me the technical training that I needed. I became skillful in my art, and, had not ambition been dead within me, might soon, I believe, have found myself on the highroad to fortune.

As it was, I worked without heart, giving my master only his due, and spending my spare time in the miserable holes and corners of the city, where those who were the makers of its wealth herded together like so many cattle. Ah! how my heart would beat within me as I looked on at the misery of my fellows. But I found more than misery, I found men who had determined that oppression should cease, whose strong arms were ready to strike when the hour should come —the men of the future! They made me one of themselves, and that I was not the least ardent spirit of that little band of dreamers mademoiselle will readily believe. And if she only knew what we knew, what we saw every day going on under our eyes—the misery, the wrong heaped upon wrong that at last drove our people mad—ah! then her pity for the misfortunes of the wrong-doers would be quenched in a pity deeper and larger far.

But, pardon me, I wander from my story. My year of apprenticeship passed away, and I, refusing all offers to remain at Lyons, returned to our quiet home, there to wait like those I left behind till our hour should come.

I found my father aged and altered. I think he was disappointed at my continued dejection, but he said little. Had the iron entered into his soul too? I sometimes wondered. If it had he never told me, nor would he be drawn into conversation on the subject nearest to my heart.

Some months went by uneventfully, perhaps nearly a year, I do not remember very distinctly. No news came of Antoinette nor of the Marquis. The steward continued to gather to the last cruel farthing what was due to his master, and that was all we ever heard of him.

One evening—it must have been in autumn, for the air was heavy with the scent of the moist earth and falling leaves—as Mother was preparing our supper at the fire, and Father and I were sitting near the open door, I heard a rustling sound outside. I got up at once, thinking that a bird had been caught in a snare, and wishing to release it. Scarcely had I done so when we saw in the dim light a white figure coming towards us.

"It is a vision of Our Lady," cried my mother, who had come to the door, and she fell on her knees. But I knew better. I did not wait to utter a word. I sprang over the fence that divided the garden from the orchard, and arrived just in time to receive in my arms our Antoinette, who in her haste had stumbled against the stump of a tree. Finding that she was in an almost insensible state, I bore her to our house, and gave her into the keeping of my mother. After a few moments, during which we watched her with the deepest anxiety, she flung her arms round my mother's neck, crying out, "Save me! Save me!"

It was strange and sweet to me to see my mother soothe her with tender words and loving gestures, even as she had done long ago when our darling was a little child crying over a hurt or an un-kindness.

She would not allow us so much as to speak to her. "Let her alone," she said, "let her alone. Leave my little one to me." Presently, seeing that Antoinette could do nothing but weep and cling to her, she took her off, and carried her to bed like a tired child.

Little by little the next day we learnt An-toinette's history. Her father had disliked her from the first, and had never ceased to treat her cruelly. His last brutality was an attempt to force her into marriage with a man she hated. When this failed he threatened to shut her up in a convent for the rest of her days. To our An-toinette, who loved the fresh air and a simple natural life, the thought of such a fate was terrible. Driven to desperation, she managed to escape, and by many devious ways—for she feared discovery—found her way to us, her old friends, whom she implored to protect her.

Little lady, I must pass over this part of my story quickly. God knows it was from no selfish motive that I listened to the promptings of my heart, and with Antoinette secretly left my parents' house, in which, as we both knew, she could not much longer be hidden. It was to save her from cruel usage, to protect her, to have the right to make her life my care, that, knowing her heart even as I knew my own, I asked her to be my wife. Together, I believed, we might defy the world. We went to Lyons, where we were married. I found employment at once with the designer whose apprentice I had been. We hired a pretty little cottage in the outskirts of the city. My darling, who said she was not born for a fine lady, took up her new position cheerfully, and a life happier far than any I had dreamed of began for us.

It was only after we were married that I told my father and mother what I had done, for I did not wish that they should share the responsibility of our deed.

I sometimes think now that dread of the punishment that might follow my rash act broke my father's heart, for he died soon afterwards, and then my mother came to us.

In the meantime the Marquis made no sign. Sometimes this very silence made me uneasy, but the present was so full of happiness that I was able to put away all fear for the future. When our first child—a little girl—was born, we felt we had nothing more to wish for. We called our little one Louise Edith, after her two grandmothers, Antoinette insisting that my mother's name should come first.

I would gladly linger over those pleasant days that went by so quickly, but I must pass on. Even then, when our child was born, the shadow that was fated to fall upon our happy home had begun to approach us. It was well for us, it may be, that we could not see it coming, else would the happiness of those few blissful months, when Antoinette, and my mother, and I, and the little one whom the good God had given us, were all the world to one another, have been darkened; for even had we foreseen the blow we could not have averted it. In those dark days there was no law for the poor man in France.

It must have been fifteen years ago this very springtime, for our spring, I remember, was coming on—the spring of the south, with its rapid, glorious wakening to life of all creation. One morning I went out to my work as usual, having first kissed my little girl and placed her in her mother's arms. I was to return early, having promised to do some little service for Antoinette.

I saw her watching me, still holding our child in her arms, till a turn in the road hid them from view. As I hastened on I experienced for the first time a feeling of impatience with my lot. It was hard, I thought, that I should have to spend so much time away from my beloved home. All through the day this feeling of impatience was upon me, and I thought the hours would never pass. My master had some orders which he was anxious to execute quickly. As I was his best workman he wished me to remain beyond my time, but I managed to excuse myself.

As I went along the familiar road which led to our cottage I was surprised by my own agitation. When, however, I came within sight of the beloved spot, and saw everything looking just as usual, I was ready to laugh at my fears. In a few moments, I thought, as I hurried on, I would be laughing over them with Antoinette.

She was not in the garden; but this was not strange, as, doubtless, she did not expect me so early. I walked up the little path, bordered on each side with sweet flowers of spring, and I thought it was curious she did not hear my step and come to greet me, as was her custom. Suddenly the extraordinary stillness of the whole place struck me. A dread which I could not have put into words fell upon my heart. I stopped for a moment listening for some sound. None reached me, and I pressed forward to the front door, which opened into our kitchen.

Ah! what a scene met my view! The room was in disorder. Antoinette—my Antoinette—whom I would have sheltered with my own life from pain or danger, was lying on the little couch, her hands and feet bound, her eyes closed, a terrible scar on her white face. My poor old mother, who tried feebly to gasp out my name, was tied with cords to her chair by the hearth. The child was nowhere to be seen.

You may imagine—you, mademoiselle, with your tender heart—what my feelings were as I looked round.

My first action was to spring to Antoinette's side, for I thought she was dead. But as I stood by her she opened her eyes. That look! how terrible it was to me! I read in it what she had suffered. I saw, as in a vision, what she would suffer—my poor, innocent angel, whose one and only crime was that she was too good, too noble, for the class to which she belonged.

She was past speaking; but she pointed to the floor, where, as I now saw, an open letter was lying. I picked it up, and this is what I read:

"It is I, your father, whom you have defied and degraded, who sends his messengers for your child. If you will not give it up quietly, they are commanded to use force; attempt to dispute my will, and the wretch you call husband shall spend the rest of his days in prison. Whether you are submissive or whether you rebel, understand this. For your disobedience to my will, for his audacity in allying himself with a member of my family, my vengeance—the vengeance of a man who was never known to forgive—will follow you both to your graves.   DE LA FONTENAYE"

Feeling like one stunned I dropped the fatal letter. Nothing was said by any of us until I had unbound my mother and Antoinette, and then in broken words my mother told me the cruel story.

About noon some masked men entered the house, and, after placing a letter in Antoinette's hand, seized the child, forced a gag into her tender mouth, and prepared to take her away. Antoinette and my mother resisted, but they were soon overpowered. It is a scene which I can never bear to picture to myself. During the struggle my mother managed to tie round the child's neck a little trinket, my only present to Antoinette, and a bag containing a few gold pieces, her own savings.

My dear mother! To the day of her death she firmly believed that by this means we should some day trace our lost little one. We all kept watch together that night, for Antoinette, who feared I might do some rash deed, would not let me out of her sight for a moment. As we thought, and tried to speak, of what had happened, it seemed to me that I could see one reason for the mysterious cruelty of the deed that had been committed.

I had heard that the property of the Marquis must descend in the direct line, even if the heir was a female; but knowing all that rank and influence can obtain, I had never doubted but that the Marquis could gain the royal permission to leave it away from a daughter who had disgraced herself by marrying a peasant. It struck me now, that if the Marquis were out of favour at court, this might not be so easy, and that he had taken away his daughter's heir, not for revenge alone, but to bring her up in the ways of his order.

I said this to Antoinette, and I think it gave her a gleam of comfort; but I can truly say it only added to my bitterness, for I would rather, I felt, have seen my child dead before me, than have had her brought up as one of the hated aristocrats. This was only the beginning of troubles. I excused myself from my work on the following day, and in the evening I received a note from the master of the works, saying that he required my services no longer. This was a crushing blow. I knew I had done nothing to deserve dismissal, and I rushed off to the town and demanded to see the master. He denied himself to me at first; but hearing from his people, I suppose, that I was nearly frantic, he admitted me for a few moments to his private room. I had not displeased him in any way, he said. I was a good workman, and he was sure I could soon get employment if I set myself to find it. For his own part, he had no choice; if he kept me he would offend patrons whom he could not afford to lose. With despair in my heart I returned home; I knew now that there would be no use in searching for work at Lyons, and we made immediate arrangements for leaving the cottage that we loved, and where we had lived so happily together. Alas! it was all in vain. Go where we would the vengeance of the terrible Marquis followed us.

No one would employ me. I did, indeed, occasionally sell my designs for small sums, and as it were by stealth; but I did not earn enough to keep us, and the little money we had laid by during the first two years of our marriage was becoming rapidly exhausted.

In the midst of these anxieties my Toinette— a sick miserable infant—came to us. I could not rejoice over her birth, but to her mother's heart, I think, she brought some consolation. After this our misery only deepened. The next great trouble came when my mother was taken from us. I missed her at every turn, and Antoinette was inconsolable. Poor soul! she had given up everything for us, and her patience, tenderness, and love never once failed, and yet—I could find it in my heart to be relieved when she was gone

—she was at peace, and I—I had one less mouth to feed. But a still heavier trial was in store for me. From the day of my mother's death, Antoinette, who had never been the same since the loss of her child, began to fail more rapidly. Her gentle spirit was broken.

I sent for a doctor, who recommended wine and nourishing food, and freedom from care. When we were outside my wife's room I laughed in his face. I would have given her my heart's blood, but I could not provide her with the bare necessaries of life!

I will not linger over that sad time. Day by day she grew feebler, at last one chill dawn she gathered all her little strength together, and prayed me to forgive her for the ruin she had brought me as her dower. Choked with agony, unable even to speak, I knelt down beside her. She smiled, commended our little one to me, and passed away to where even the vengeance of a great Noble could not follow her.

There is little more to tell. The battle I had to wage was fierce, but my arm never failed. As years went on, the Noble Marquis, I suppose, forgot me, for his persecution ceased. I found employment, and came to Paris.

Then the great struggle began, and you, mademoiselle, know something of what happened. What you do not know is, that when, after Toinette was taken from me, I saw the wild work of the mob, my soul began to sicken within me. That the power which the Nobles had so basely used should be taken from them, that the

people should govern with equity and right—
this was my dream—not a reign of murder and
violence.

One day, shortly after Toinette's death, I went
into the prison where the aristocrats were con-
fined. I forget what took me there, but I think
I had been sent for by one of the prisoners, who
had been acquainted with me formerly. On my
way I came across a broken-down, half-childish
old man, whose face seemed known to me. For
a few moments I stood looking at him, then
suddenly I remembered where I had seen him
before. It was my enemy, the Marquis de la
Fontenaye, whom I had so strangely found.

Ah! mademoiselle, you will imagine how, as I
gazed at him, the memory of the past would
rush back to my mind! I went away, and by the
wrongs I had suffered, claimed of the revolutionary tribunal that I should be allowed to
dispose of his fate.

My demand was granted, I returned to the
prison, and saw the Marquis again. If he was
my enemy, he was an enemy now unworthy
even of my hatred. He did not remember me;
all his talk was of old times and the court, and
his distressing want of toilet.

I spent many days with him, for I was de-
voured with anxiety to know if my first-born
still lived, but I could get nothing reasonable
from him. At last he grew so feeble that he
took to his bed. One morning, when I went to
pay him my daily visit, I found him altered.
He did not speak when I entered, but he fixed his

cold eyes scrutinizingly upon mine, and I saw that he knew me.

"So," he said at last, "your turn has come. What do you want of me?"

"My child, your granddaughter," I answered.

A look of triumph passed over his face.

"Good!" he cried; "my vengeance follows you still! Your child? You will never find her; she was taken to England years ago, and there she may have died for aught I know."

Upon this my passion almost mastered me. I approached him; he raised himself with a great effort.

"You dared," he shrieked, "to mingle your vile blood with the noblest in France, you—" He raised his withered hand to strike me, and fell back— dead. So my vengeance escaped me, and all chance of finding my child was gone. I returned home with a determination to mix no more in the dreadful scenes around me. I even ventured to assist those in distress. Having been concerned in the escape of a Noble family I found myself looked upon with suspicion, and I saw my only safety was in flight. I gathered together my little savings, and weary and hopeless I came to England, still with the vague idea of searching for my daughter.

The rest, mademoiselle, you know. When you recognized me my last sou was spent. I thought the world was over for me—I was almost gone. But I think I understand now that the good God in His mercy will keep me here a little longer, till I am more worthy to rejoin my angels in His Paradise. The mysteries of this world

M. JACQUES VISITS THE MARQUIS IN PRISON

have troubled me overmuch hitherto. In my anxiety to set them right I have gone nigh to shedding innocent blood. But I have learned my lesson. Henceforth I will try to believe that the Great Father in His good time will make all things straight, and though I am, and must always be, M. Jacques the republican, I am thankful that He has permitted me to know that sometimes Noble blood is dignified by union with noble hearts.

CHAPTER XV

MARIE'S STORY CONTINUED

MAY 25th—When I had finished writing M. Jacques' story at his dictation, Father said he should like Mother to hear it; so two evenings ago, after Louis had gone to bed, M. Jacques came down to the parlour for the first time, as we wished him to be present while I read aloud what I had written. Father himself helped him downstairs, for he is still very weak, and Mother met him at the parlour door and took him by the hand and welcomed him, making him sit in an easy-chair and drink a dish of tea before doing anything else.

I know all this was a little effort to Mother, who did not want to hear M. Jacques' story; for though she had forgiven him with all her heart, and strove to remember only the service he rendered us, she dreaded a reopening of the past.

I, on the contrary, was certain that when she knew his history her feelings towards him would undergo an alteration, and presently I took up my precious book, and having first asked Mother's permission I began to read. Father knew most of the story before, but to Mother it was a revelation. Before I had finished reading the tears were running down her face, and when I had ended she rose and took M. Jacques' hand.

"You asked my forgiveness once," she said, "I ask yours now."

"Madame—?" stammered M. Jacques.

"Yes," she said; and it was strange to see Mother so much moved. "I judged you harshly. I thought I was doing a great deed in forgiving you. I little dreamt of what your wounds had been. May God forgive me!" she added in her usual tone. "May He comfort you, my poor friend!"

Since that evening Mother and M. Jacques seem to have understood one another in a wonderful way. She has persuaded him that he can be of great service to Louis, who is fast forgetting his French tongue; and now these two talk French together every day. He is as careful and gentle with Louis as even we could be, never allowing the conversation to wander to any exciting topics, and amusing him in many ways that would never occur to us.

It is sad to see this strong man, who was of so high a spirit, as he is now, patient and humble towards us all, and grateful for the smallest kindness. I am afraid he feels that life is over for him, and I sometimes think that it is almost as hard to him to live as it is to others to die. But my father says that he is young still, not forty, and that he may yet make for himself a happy and prosperous career.

Father, who thinks that his talent for designing is remarkable, has obtained several orders for him already, but of these we have as yet told him nothing. He is still weak and wants care, and he would not stay with us if he thought there was work to be done.

Our dear Louis' health meanwhile does not improve as we could wish. His blue eyes have grown larger, and his cheeks look thin and white, except when they burn with fever. My father is of opinion that it would be well for us to return with him to the country; but the London doctors persuade my mother that they can still do something for him if he remains in town. This dreadful anxiety about Louis seems like a blight poisoning all our pleasures. I, in addition to this, have another sorrow. Through all these weeks and days there has been never a word about Edith—not the slightest clue by the aid of which we might pursue our search. Sometimes now I give up hope. I say to myself that she is dead— that never again in this world shall I see the friend whom I loved so dearly.

To return to M. Jacques. I must put down, before I forget, that we have found out, in rather a strange way, that he and my father and mother have mutual friends. He spoke in his story of having rescued a French family. My father, being naturally interested in everything relating to France, asked their name. M. Jacques mentioned it readily, giving at the same time the address of the poor lodging in Islington where they are waiting for better times, and where, until his money was completely exhausted, he used to go now and then to see them.

It turns out that when we lived in Paris my father and mother, who were much about the court, knew this exiled family very well, as they also had been in frequent attendance on the King and Queen. Alas! what a change! From the Tuileries and Versailles to a poor little lodging in Islington! The thought of this has touched my mother's heart, and she is filled with a desire to be of service to them. It is arranged that we shall pay them a visit tomorrow.

May 26th—Thank God! thank God! My heart is singing for joy—running over with thankfulness. I hardly know how to sit still and write. But in this journal, which contains the account of my sorrow, I ought also to record my joy. I must try therefore to sit down soberly and write down everything that has occurred. When M. Jacques spoke about the French family, how little did any of us foresee what would come of it!

Yesterday—can it be but yesterday?—my mother and I set off in the coach to pay our visit. The drive seemed long, to me at least; for—selfish that I am—I was a little impatient at being taken away from home when M. Jacques was talking to Louis and telling him some wonderful stories.

At last, however, we rattled into stony Islington, and drew up before a poor little house, with a small front garden looking on the street. Two children were playing in the garden, under the care apparently of an older person; but as they were led away at once I did not see what they were like.

The servant who answered our knock led the way upstairs, and showed us into a poor dingy little sitting-room, with faded carpet and shabby furniture and hangings. Here Madame de Vignon, and her daughter, Madame de Ville, were sitting at their embroidery frames. Poor as the room was they showed no embarrassment. They received us with as much grace and self-possession as if they had been in their own beautiful château. I could just recall having seen the old Marquise one day at Versailles, when she patted me on the head and praised Louis' looks. Then she was beautifully dressed, and was the centre of a brilliant throng—for she was famous for her wit, Mother says—now she had on a poor black gown, her hair was gray, and her figure bent; but, changed as she was, no one could approach her without knowing her to be a great lady still.

She held out both her hands to receive my mother, and for a moment I thought her emotion would conquer her, but she fought it down, and, after the first few instants of silence, one might have thought that this was but an ordinary meeting.

By degrees the conversation began to run easily. Madame de Vignon told my mother of their happy escape from Paris, and mentioned M. Jacques' name, speaking graciously of the help he had given them. He was an excellent person, she said, with good intentions. I could see, however, that she considered him to have been amply repaid for the services he had rendered them by the honour of helping a family of quality in distress. "When we return to France the Marquis will reward him," she said. There the subject dropped. Mother now turned to Madame de Ville, and asked her about her children. Madame de Ville had lost her husband in the Revolution, and she seemed much more broken down than the Marquise. After replying to Mother's questions she said:

"Speaking of my children reminds me of a service M. Jacques rendered us lately. He found a young girl wandering about London with only a louis d'or in her pocket, and he brought her to us, begging us to protect her. It was a strange request; but after what we owed him we did not like to refuse, and we consented that she should come to us for a few days. This happened some months ago, and she is still with us. I found her so useful, and her ways so gentle, that I have taken her on as my children's *gouvernante*. My mother was against it at first, but—"

"Yes, but I have given in," interrupted the old lady nodding. "There is some mystery; I said so from the beginning, and I say the same now, for there can be no doubt that the young girl is a gentlewoman. But we who have seen so many reverses—" and she sighed and glanced at my mother, who gave a sad sympathetic smile, and said nothing could be stranger than what she and the Marquise had seen.

After this there was some further talk about former days, and then my mother asked if she might not see the children and their gouvernante, whereupon Madame de Ville went to fetch them. She came back in a few minutes leading a little girl in each hand; but my eyes did not rest on them for a second, they went further, and fell on the gouvernante, who followed modestly, her eyes on the ground.

Wonder of wonders! I recognized her. For

an instant I stood hesitating. It seemed too great—too strange a thing to happen thus. I might be mistaken, perhaps it was only a chance resemblance. Then like a flash of lightning the whole story darted upon me. The desolate girl —the single louis d'or—the silence—the reserve— the gentleness. Ah! it takes long to write, the pen is so slow, it cannot put down everything in a moment. It did not take me long to think. Before I knew where I was, or what I was doing, I had run to her and flung my arms round her neck. "Edith!" I cried, "Edith, do you not know me? I am Marie, your friend."

Edith did not return my embrace, she drew herself away; with a little cry of distress she hid her face in her hands, and rushed from the room. Did she not know me then? Had she forgotten all our happy days together? The thought made me tremble, and, forgetting that we were not in our own house, I was about to follow her, when my mother laid her hand upon my arm.

"Marie," she said, "you cannot go to Edith without first asking the permission of Madame la Marquise. If she will excuse you, you can go, and I will explain the cause of your excitement to her."

Here kind Madame de Ville came to my assistance.

"Come with me," she said gently; "since madame your mother consents we shall be delighted for you to see the poor child. So you know her. She is your friend. That is good news for us all." Talking thus she led the way up some crooked stairs to a little scantily furnished upper chamber. On the bed lay my dearest Edith, sobbing as if her heart would break.

"My child," said Madame de Ville kindly, "I have brought an old friend to see you. Will you not look up and bid her welcome?"

As for me, I was trembling so much that I could hardly stand. I knelt down beside the bed, and put my arms round my Edith's neck. It was impossible for me to speak, and she was no better, and for a few minutes we cried together. Then after smiling at me encouragingly Madame de Ville left us alone.

Edith was the first to speak, but her voice was broken with sobs.

"I will never go back," she cried, "not even for you, Marie, never."

"Dearest Edith," I answered, "do you think I should ever ask you to go back? Have you nothing else to say to me after our long parting? Are you sorry to see me again?"

"Sorry!" she exclaimed. "Oh, Marie, if you knew how I have thought of you, how I have longed for the sound of your voice, for one of your mother's loving looks!"

"Dear," I said soothingly, "we all love you as much as ever. You will come to us now, and never leave us again."

"Marie," said Edith, with some of the old defiance in her face and manner, "if you love me, never speak of that again. I listened to you once, and brought disgrace and unhappiness on your home. I am independent now, and I am happy because I earn my bread; Madame de Ville is very kind, and I love the children. Kiss me and say goodbye; I shall never forget any of you, but I do not belong to you. Since I have been here I have learned that a gulf lies between the great and wellborn and such as I." As Edith spoke these words her look startled me, it was so strangely like an expression I had seen on M. Jacques' face when he spoke of the wicked Marquis.

"Oh!" I cried, "are such miserable things as these to come between us? I love you, Edith, you are my sister. You must come back to us."

She remained firm, however, and in the end I was obliged to promise that I would not try to induce her to leave Madame de Ville. After this she became gentle and affectionate, and we talked together freely. I told her about Louis, for whom I saw she longed yet feared to ask, making as light of his illness as I dared; then, after another loving embrace to make sure it was really my Edith whom I had found, fearing we had already been absent too long, we went down hand in hand to the little drawing-room. Mother saw, I think, that we could neither of us bear many words just then, and though, as I could see, her heart was full, she contented herself with smiling at me, and kissing Edith warmly. After this the marquise patted her on the head, and said she was charmed to find that their little maiden had such good friends; Madame de Ville pressed her hand, and then my poor Edith, who seemed almost overcome at the meeting with my mother, asked for permission to return to the children. This, however, we would not allow her to do till it was arranged that she should spend the next day with us.

Happy and thankful as I was, no sooner were we safely in the coach than I began sobbing and crying as if, Mother said, trying to make me smile, some great calamity had happened to us; and indeed I did not know why I was crying—it was because I was so happy I said, which was certainly not very wise. Mother held my hand and soothed me, saying, I must show a bright face to Father and Louis, for no one but myself should tell them of our wonderful discovery. When I reached home I did try to tell them, but the words I wanted would not come. Mother came to my help once more, and finally she took me to my room and sat by me till I slept.

This morning some of my first excitement had gone, and I was able to think and speak calmly. Edith came towards noon. To tell of how we received her, of what she said and did, of how Louis' face beamed with pleasure, of how even M. Jacques, who did not know her as we did, but who had helped her in her distress, was moved and interested—all this would take volumes.

A day is a very short time to be together when friends have been parted so long, and though we made the best of the hours that were given to us, we could not hear and relate everything. Edith and I have arranged, therefore, that I shall lend her this book—my precious journal—and that after reading what I have written she shall write down in it the story of her wanderings.

Louis, who says he wishes to make the acquaintance of the Marquise and Madame de Ville, and Edith's little charges, will ride to Islington tomorrow, and take my book with him.

CHAPTER XVI

EDITH'S STORY

MARIE will persist in making much of my adventures, and nothing will satisfy her but that I shall write down in this book everything that happened since we parted. To hear her talk, one would think I was a heroine of romance, instead of a poor nameless girl, driven out into the wide world to seek a home. However, as she wishes it, I will tell my little story as well as I can.

Oh! the burning sense of wrong and humiliation that filled my heart when, after I had struck Tom, I became suddenly aware of what I had done. True, I had received great and bitter provocation. Cruelty to myself I could have borne —I was used to it—but cruelty towards my dearest friends, my benefactors, roused me to passionate anger. Still, mine was not the hand that should have struck the blow. The moment I realized what I had done, and saw how people looked at me, and heard my aunt's cries, my anger gave place to shame and remorse.

As I stood in my place, the bow of the fiddle still in my hand, with all eyes turned upon me, a plan which had long been floating vaguely through my mind took form. I would run away; I would have done with the life I was leading; I would make a place for myself in the world. While I stood there, to all appearance sullen and defiant, I was making my plans. I determined to go home quietly with my aunt, to face her rage as best I could, and, when all was over and the house was still, to take my five gold pieces and escape.

I glanced at you, my Marie, your face was white and your lips trembled, but you were trying bravely to take your mother's place with the guests. She, my dear Mrs. Hamilton, was watching beside Louis. I was thankful that you were both too much occupied to notice me.

One loving parting look I gave to Marie, then I stole upstairs and crept along the corridor until I reached the door of Louis' room. How I longed to enter, to throw my arms round Mrs. Hamilton's neck, and ask her to pardon my violence! But I remembered that I was nothing to her. If I had been her own child I might have claimed her forgiveness, I might have entreated to share her watch. But I was nothing, nothing to her, nothing to any of them. They had been kind to me, they had been touched by my desolate position, they had allowed me to take part in their joys; but I was not of their kin, and from their sorrows I was shut out. I bent down and kissed the threshold where I knelt, and though my lips could frame no prayer, my heart implored a blessing upon those to whom I was bidding farewell silently, and, as I thought, forever. Then, trying to be courageous, I went quietly downstairs again, and hid myself behind one of the pillars in the hall to wait for my aunt. She came out very soon, followed by Tom, who muttered savagely, and I jumped into the carriage after them. I tried to say a few words of apology to my aunt; she listened to me in complete silence, and I began to think nothing more would be said that night.

But I was greatly mistaken. After we had entered the house, just as I put my foot on the stairs leading to my room, I received a blow on my head from Tom. His brutality was no new thing to me, and on this occasion I would have borne it in silence, but Mrs. Sinclair rushed forward, seized me by the arm, and dragged me into her parlour, where she poured forth such a torrent of reproaches as even I had never heard from her before. I was dizzy with pain, stupid with fatigue, and, happily no doubt for myself, I only heard part of what she said. I believe she told me that she was not my aunt, that she was in fact no relation of mine; this I was able to take in, and I try to remember nothing else. When her passion had run its course, she was more exhausted than I had ever seen her, and she then bade me go to my room and not leave it until I was sent for.

Thankful, very thankful I was to obey her. My head was swimming, and I was in pain all over, but I never once swerved from my resolve. "It is for the last time—the last time," I repeated over and over to myself, and this thought gave me strength to endure.

When I was alone in my room at last, I stripped off the beautiful dress I had put on with such pride and joy only a few short hours before, put out my light, and kept quite still until all was quiet in the house. When I was sure that everything was safe I dressed myself in my oldest and shabbiest clothes, tied a few little gifts of Mrs. Hamilton's and Marie's in a bundle, and with my locket pressed against my heart, and my gold pieces hidden in my dress, opened my door and stole downstairs.

My plan was to unfasten the parlour window and let myself out that way, for I thought it would make less noise than loosening the bolts and bars of the front door. I succeeded, but I had one terrible moment. How it happened I cannot tell; I suppose I must have been exhausted by all I had gone through during the day. As I was lifting the shutter bar it dropped from my fingers and fell to the ground. At the noise Tom's bulldog began to bark; I was sure that the house would be aroused, and in my terror— I had lost all power over myself—I crouched down in a corner, lifting up my hands to ward off the blows that I fancied were certain to fall upon me; nothing stirred, however, and I took heart again.

In a few moments I was outside. Dark as it was, I reached the garden gate without accident, and soon found myself in the village street. As

my eyes grew accustomed to the darkness I
went on more rapidly, the intense cold, of which I
was hardly conscious, keeping away all sense of
fatigue. For some time I walked on quickly,
then at last I stopped, drew a long breath and
looked around me. The village was far behind;
the place where I stood was as silent as a desert.
I was free—free! By the faint light which began
to peep in the east I saw that the sky was of a
heavy lurid gray. The air also was bitterly cold,
though very still. In a few moments snow began
to fall, at first in large slowly-dropping flakes,
then more and more thickly and rapidly, till I
could scarcely see where I was going. But still
I plodded on. How far I had gone, when fatigue
and a sense of despair began to overcome me, I
cannot tell; but there came a moment at last
when I felt I could walk no further. My clothes
were heavy with snow, my shoes were so clogged
with wet that I could scarcely move in them, and
my head began to feel dizzy again.

Longing to rest, if only for a few minutes, I
sat down under a high hedge which sheltered me
a little from the bitter wind. When I had been
there for a short time, a gradual and increasing
drowsiness came over me. It was not at all unpleasant, though I had a feeling that it would be
dangerous to give way, and indeed, for the first
few instants, I did try to fight against it. But
fighting was in vain. I soon lost all power over
myself, I was slipping away, forgetting everything, floating calmly over strange and beautiful
seas, when suddenly a familiar noise fell upon
my ear, and, roused from my trance, I sprang

up and looked round me. The noise was the barking of Tom's dog. Whether the stillness of the air had carried the sound from Mrs. Sinclair's house to where I lay, or whether anyone was in search of me, I do not know. But of this I am sure. If I had not been awakened, and awakened violently, that sleep under the hedge would have been my last. When I heard the sound and started up, I was half-buried with snow.

My first thought was that I was being pursued, and I went on as quickly as I could, keeping close to the hedge so that I might not be traced by the marks of my footsteps along the road. My plan was to walk on if I could until I came to the next posting-town, to rest at an inn there, and to take the first coach to London, where, as I hoped, I might find work to keep me from starving after my gold pieces were spent. By this time morning had come. It was a dull and dreary dawn, showing me nothing but fields upon fields of snow, but happily for me the highroad, which was bounded by tall hedges, could not easily be mistaken. I went on and on. I passed through several villages. I saw men going out to their work, and I longed more than once to go into a cottage and ask for shelter and food; but I dared not; I might, I thought, be found and brought back to the dreadful life I was leaving.

The morning advanced, and when at length I reached the first posting-town on the road, ten o'clock was chiming from the church-tower. I was still very much afraid of being caught, but I knew that I could not go on further without rest and food, so I left the highroad, turned down a small side street, and, with the courage of despair, knocked at the door of the first inn I came to.

An elderly woman of pleasant appearance came out.

"What is thy errand, my lass?" she cried, looking at me with the greatest surprise, and then she put out her hand and drew me in. "Who could have had the heart to send thee abroad on such a morning?" she went on.

I tried to reply, but my voice died away, and I knew no more until I found myself lying before a great fire, my wet outer garments removed, and some one gently chafing my swollen hands. I did not know where I was, and I did not care to inquire, the delicious sense of warmth and comfort was all I could take in just then.

Presently I heard a kind voice say:

"She's for all the world like our Hetty, John."

I opened my eyes, and saw a rough-looking man bending over me, but his face was so good and honest that it did not alarm me in the least.

"The lass has come to already, wife," said the man. "Here, my pretty! drink this and lie quiet."

I did as I was bid, and by degrees my scattered senses returned, so that I was able to remember where I was, and what had brought me thither. My first movement was to feel for my gold pieces, which were safe; then I sat up and looked round me. As I saw how comfortable and homely the room was, and met the kind anxious gaze of my new friends, my courage revived. "Surely," I said to myself, "it is the Lord who has brought me hither."

In answer to their anxious questions, I told them that I was quite well again; then, after having thanked them as well as I could for all they had done for me, I begged them to let me get up at once, as I must take the next coach for London.

"London!" they exclaimed both together. "But that will be impossible," added the man. "If the coach starts today it will not go far."

I said that I must go, and they appeared to give in. When, however, they had given me something to eat, they left the room, and I overheard a whispered conversation going on outside the door. I felt sure that they were talking about me, and was half-inclined—I was so afraid of being given back to Mrs. Sinclair—to run away; but I was only partly dressed, and I felt too weak to do anything desperate. So, though my heart was beating fast, I sat still and waited. When they returned, I asked as calmly as I could at what hour the coach was expected to start.

"About one o' the clock," answered the man shortly, and then his dear good wife came and laid her hand on my shoulder. "My lass," she said, "do not take it ill that I ask thee; but is it any good that takes thee to London in such weather?"

A great temptation seized me to say what was not true, to tell her of a sick mother or brother who was waiting for me in London, for I thought that these simple folk would readily believe such a story. But before the words were spoken I remembered Mrs. Hamilton and Marie, and I determined that, come what might, I would not stoop to a lie. So, after a moment's pause, I answered quickly that I believed I was going for a good purpose. The woman shook her head. "Little lass," she said, "I had a daughter once. The Lord took her away from us just a year ago last Christmastime. Thou hast a face like hers, and I cannot stand by and see thee go astray. In the name of our Hetty I ask thee to tell me what thou wouldst do in London?"

As she spoke she looked at me earnestly, and as the man too bent forward I almost fancied I saw tears in his eyes. Their goodness touched me to the heart. "I will tell you," I said, "I will tell you everything."

Hastily then, for the time was short, I told my story, only concealing my name and that of Mrs. Sinclair, and I ended by throwing my arms round the woman's neck and imploring her not to stop me. How I managed to persuade them to take my view of the case I do not know, though I remember pouring out what seemed to me most convincing arguments.

They gave in at last, and promised to keep my secret, even to assist me, on the condition that, when I arrived in London, I would go straight to some relations of theirs, to whom they were to give me a letter, and who, they promised, would provide me with shelter until I could find something to do.

I now brought out my gold pieces and asked what I should do about them, for I knew they were not English gold, and I had no idea of their value. The man, who turned them over curiously, did not understand them at all; he said, however, that he thought he might exchange them in the town, and I gave four of the pieces into his keeping. I wanted to keep one of them if possible, as my old nurse had told me that she believed they had belonged to my mother.

He went out immediately, and returned after a very short delay looking very cheerful indeed. A seafaring neighbour, who was about to start on another journey, had said that they were gold pieces, current in France, and had given him in exchange for them a sum of English money large enough to pay the whole of my journey to London, and something over.

About noon the weather cleared, and my kind friends seeing this grew more reconciled to the idea of allowing me to go. They provided me with a small basket, containing a pasty and some cakes, and a warm shawl that had been Hetty's. They refused also to take any payment for what they had done, bidding me keep my money for my further needs; and when the time for starting was at hand they walked with me through the town, placed me in the coach, and begged the guard to look after me, as I was a friend of theirs.

"Goodbye, little lass," whispered the woman, "the Lord go with thee!" I could not speak my thanks. I felt as if they were my dear friends, and it rent my heart to part with them. Yet how much happier I was than I had been before I found them! The world seemed a better place for their goodness; the lamp of love had shone on my dark way, and Hetty's shawl about my neck was like the warmth of loving arms.

When we were fairly off I settled myself into a corner of the coach, and being very tired fell asleep almost directly. I must have slept for some time; for when, aroused by a sudden jolt, I started up darkness had fallen. At first I was very much perplexed, and could not remember where I was; but the rush of cold air that came into the coach, and the voice of the guard, who threw open the door and bade us alight as we were stuck fast in the snow, recalled me to myself.

I had been too much exhausted on starting to take any notice of my fellow-passengers. I found now that there were only three besides myself, and that they were all men. They were kind to me after a rough fashion, and a shelter of tarpaulins was made for me hastily on the snow; but when the guard muttered that lasses should bide at home in such weather, I think they all agreed with him.

They now turned their attention to the coach, which was firmly embedded in the snow. All their efforts to move it proved useless, and at last a passenger of a more adventurous mind than the rest proposed to take one of the coach lamps and go off in search of a village or farmhouse. The coachman offered to go with him, and away they started into the darkness, while we who were left behind were glad to take refuge in the coach again.

Hours seemed to go by. At last, when I was

so numb with cold that I could scarcely feel anything, and my fellow-passengers were giving
themselves up for lost, we heard the sound of
loud shouting in the distance, and in a very few
minutes we were surrounded by what seemed
like a little army of men carrying flaming torches
and spades and pickaxes. By their united efforts
we were soon set free, and then a number of them
went before the coach, cutting a road for it
through the heaped-up snow. Our progress was
very slow, and before we reached our halting-
place, a roadside inn in a small village, the day
—my second day of freedom—had begun to
dawn.

That terrible storm lasted for two days, and
during the whole of that time it was impossible
for us to go on. I hired a little room, where I
remained alone, busy with the sad thoughts
which filled my mind now that I was able to
think again. And indeed I had many things to
think of. I thought of you, Marie, of Louis,
whom I had last seen so pale and ill, and of Mrs.
Hamilton and her deep anxiety. Kneeling down,
I poured out earnest prayers to our Father in
heaven that He would forgive me for having
brought unhappiness into your beautiful home,
and that He would turn your sorrow into joy.

I could not help thinking, too, about how Marie
would grieve when she found that I was gone.
As I looked out from the window of my little
room over the waste of snow, and remembered
the dangers I had met with in my flight, it came
to me as a thought which had comfort in it that
my friends would think I was dead. They would

search for me most likely, and they would be sorry for my hard fate, and Marie, perhaps Louis also, would miss me for many a long day; but in the end they would be comforted for me and for themselves.

I lived very frugally during these two days—only eating what was absolutely necessary—and when the morning of our departure came I was shocked to find that after I had paid what I owed at the inn all my English money, except a few shillings, would be gone. I did not understand how this could be, and I was afraid to make any remark. I went on my way with a very heavy heart. Before I reached London my heart was heavier and my purse was lighter; all I possessed when we rolled over London Bridge was the gold piece which I had not changed. This I had hoped to keep as one of the last memorials of my dead mother, but I saw that to do so would be impossible, and with a sinking heart I determined to get it changed as soon as I reached the inn.

I cannot express how strange I felt, how little and how forlorn, as from my corner in the coach, which had been a sort of home to me, but which I would soon have to leave, I watched the streams of people hurrying by. While I was watching and wondering we passed under a large archway and entered the courtyard of an inn. We were quickly surrounded by a crowd of people, who were full of eager inquiries about the state of the country, for the great storm had delayed all the coaches, and it was even feared that some serious accidents had happened.

I stepped out with my little bundle, and stood by quietly until the worst of the noise and bustle were over, then, trembling very much, I went into the inn and asked a woman who appeared to be its mistress if I could have a glass of milk and some bread. At the same time I took out my gold piece, saying that it was French gold and all the money I had, and asking if she could change it for me into English silver.

My heart sank as I looked up at the woman, who had cold, cruel eyes and a coarse face. She gazed at me for a few moments silently.

"A pretty strange tale!" she said at last. "Pray, my young mistress, did you arrive by the coach?" Her voice was so loud that it attracted the attention of the men who were standing about.

"Oh! it does not matter!" I said nervously, seeing myself the centre of a number of eyes, "I can get it changed somewhere else. Good-morning!" whereupon the woman stretched out her hand and took the gold piece from me.

"Stop!" she said, "we will see what this means. Here, let me have a look at it. John!" she called out to a man in the yard, "come here. There's a young mistress come up to London with a bit of foreign gold in her pocket. She wants thee to exchange it for good English money!"

There was a little laugh amongst the bystanders, and John, who was, I suppose, the husband of the woman, came forward, took the gold piece from her hand, and examined it curiously. As he did not look unkind I thought I would appeal to him.

"Sir," I said, "I am sorry to have been troublesome. Pray, give me back my money and let me go." He glanced at his wife, who interposed hastily.

"John, thou art a fool! Let us hear where the girl comes from and whither she is going."

"Nay, nay, mistress," said a man who was standing by, "that is no business of thine. Give the girl back her gold, and let her go."

"Peace, fool'" cried the woman, turning on him angrily. "Mind thine own matters, and let honest folks mind theirs."

Hoping to put an end to this argument, I took out the letter which my friends had given me.

"This is the address to which I am going," I said. "If you will allow some one to show me the way, I will gladly pay his hire."

The woman put out her hand and would have taken the letter from me, but being on my guard I held it firmly, which, I think, annoyed her, for she called out sharply to her husband to read what was written.

"I will tell you," I said, and I read aloud—

> *"Mr. Thomas Brown,*
> *12 Paradise Row,*
> *London."*

This was greeted by a loud laugh, and the woman called out mockingly:

"Paradise Row, London! That is a good joke; and who is going to look for Paradise Row in all London, pray? It's my opinion we had better see the inside of that letter. What if this were a foreign spy?"

It was at this moment, when, trembling and

almost weeping, for I felt myself in the power of
these people, I was beginning to plead for permission to go on my way, that a tall, shabbily-
dressed man, with a dark, fierce face, pushed his
way through the little crowd, and, speaking
with a strong foreign accent, demanded to know
what the matter was.

"Matter enough," said the woman, "when
rogues come over to our country, and seek to rob
us of our hard earnings. But what is that to
thee?"

"Softly, good mistress," answered this man;
"as I take it, 'tis thou who art the thief."

"I a thief, I!" shrieked the woman.

"Aye, aye! where is the young woman's gold?"
said he.

As he spoke he looked at me, and I thought it
strange that, in spite of his rough appearance, I
did not fear him. On the contrary, my courage
began to revive, and when he asked me if it was
true that I had come there with a gold piece, I
answered boldly:

"Yes, sir; a French piece. I wished to change
it for English money."

Upon this he addressed the mistress of the inn,
who had been bandying words with the bystanders. "Be pleased to show me the young
woman's gold," he said with authority.

She might doubtless have told him to mind
his own business, but her husband interposed.
"What, wife, what?" he said. "Wouldst thou
keep the gold? It's like enough the mossoo will
know its worth; give it up to him."

The strange man took the money, examined it,

and let it lie for a moment in the palm of his hand. Seeing his hesitation, the mistress of the inn gave a little triumphant laugh. But he checked her at once. "Madame," he said, "this is a louis d'or. If mademoiselle desires to part with it I shall be happy to give her its value," and he hastily poured into my hand a quantity of silver. Then, before the woman could recover from her surprise, he took me by the arm, and whispering, "Come, my child, do not trust that bad woman," he led me away.

Neither of us spoke till we were at a safe distance from the inn. I was too much surprised, too much relieved, to say anything. I think I must have been made weaker by what I had undergone during my flight, for no sooner did I realize that I had escaped from the cruel people at the inn, and that the tall, grave man who walked beside me was my friend, than I found it impossible to control myself. I began to weep, and, do what I would, I could not stop myself. Never shall I forget how kind he was to me. "Weep on," he said gently, "if it does thy heart good. I have had little ones of my own, and I know that to the young tears are sometimes a relief."

I looked up in his face, and, rough as he was, with his poor clothes and his eyes that could look so fierce, I envied his little ones. They had someone to care for them. He told me now to call him M. Jacques, and wished to know what my name was. I said I was called Edith. "Ah!" he replied, "how strange! That is a name dear to me, and brings back many memories."

By this time we had traversed some little distance together. I had gone on with him quite naturally, because I felt from the first that I could trust him; but remembering suddenly that he was a perfect stranger to me, I stopped short and begged him not to come out of his way.

"My way is your way, mademoiselle," he answered, as courteously as the finest gentleman in the land could have done; and then, for he thought, no doubt, that I was faint and hungry, he besought me to come into a coffee-house which was close at hand and to break my fast. I agreed, partly, I think, because I had no strength to refuse, and we went in together.

Truly I had scarcely known how faint and hungry I was until I began to eat. My courage now revived, and I soon felt equal to face the world alone again; but M. Jacques, to whom I had told a great part of my story, refused to leave me till I had found the people to whose care I had been recommended by my good friends on the road.

He did not, I think, know much more of London than I did. We made inquiries before leaving the coffee-house about Paradise Row, and we were sent to a row of houses about a mile distant from where we then were. There must, however, be many Paradise Rows in London, for neither these houses, nor others to which we were directed, proved to be the right ones. At last, when we had wandered about for some time, M. Jacques said that we must hire a hackney-coach. "If there are twenty Paradise Rows in London we will go to them all," he said cheerfully, "and we must come at last to the one we want."

But hour after hour went by, and still our search was in vain. It began to grow dark, and I saw my good friend looking at me anxiously. "My child," he said, "I fear we must for this night give up our search."

"But what am I to do?" I cried, my heart sinking.

He was silent for a few moments, seeming to think. During that pause I remembered what I was doing, and how this kind man was a perfect stranger to me, and I cried out, "Oh! sir, it is wrong of me to trouble you. Pray, stop the coach, and let me get out. I will find a lodging for the night."

"And what if you find another such woman as the one you ran away from this morning?" said M. Jacques smiling. "No, no, *mon enfant*, you are not yet old enough or wise enough to be alone in London. As for trouble! if I had such trouble every day I should be a happier man. I was merely trying to consider what was best to be done, and I have hit upon a plan. I have the honour to be acquainted with two Noble ladies of France. I helped them to escape from our country when to remain there would have been dangerous, and therefore, I believe, I may ask them a favour. For one night at least I am sure they will allow you to rest at their house, and afterwards we can see what may be done."

Without waiting for my reply he told the coachman to drive to Islington; thus was my fate taken out of my own hands, and thus it strangely came about that I met my dearest friends again.

The ladies, Madame la Marquise and Madame de Ville, were very kind to me. They would not let me go away on the day after my arrival, though I wished to do so. I tried to do little services for them to show my gratitude. Madame la Marquise was hard to please at first, and even seemed to watch me, as if she suspected me of being something different from what I appeared to be; but Madame de Ville was always kind and gentle, and always pleased with what I did for her.

This went on for several days; at last Madame la Marquise began to think better of me, and I was sometimes asked to amuse the children, to whom I had not at first been allowed to speak. They took to me, dear little things! and one day —it was a proud day for me—Madame de Ville said that if I would be content with the small salary she could afford, she would like me to remain with her as the children's *gouvernante.* Content! I was more than content, I was happy. Now, for the first time in all my life, I felt independent. The next few months passed by very swiftly. I was always with the children, and I saw no one outside the house but M. Jacques, whose visits were my greatest pleasure. I had very little opportunity of speaking to him, but I liked to look at him and to listen to his voice, and when he called me *"mon enfant"* my heart went out to him, and I longed to throw my arms round his neck, and to tell him that I would indeed be his child. As time went on, however, his visits became rarer, and at last, to my great distress, they ceased altogether.

This is all I have to tell you; I will not speak
of my joy at meeting my dearest Marie and her
mother, nor of my foolish terror lest I should be
forced to return to Mrs. Sinclair.

That the Lord has indeed led me thus far I
dare to believe, and I try hard to trust in Him, and
to put away my longings for the good things
that have been denied me in this world. When
my heart grows sore with the dull aching pain of
loneliness, I picture to myself the bright Home
our dear Lord has purchased for us by His sufferings, and I know that there I shall find the love
that I have missed on earth. It is strange that
when I dream thus the face of M. Jacques mingles
ever with my dreams.

CHAPTER XVII

MARIE'S STORY—A FRESH SURPRISE

AUGUST 1st—The most wonderful part of the story is left after all for me to tell.

After the strange and happy accident which led to the discovery of our dear Edith we met frequently. She was again, as she had been in the old days, my dearest friend and Louis' play-fellow, while the sad story of her wrongs and her sufferings drew her closer than ever to Mother's heart; and yet—I must confess the truth—my Edith, the Edith to whom I used to tell my inmost thoughts, had not come back to me. It was a difference which I could feel, but which I could not define, and though I tried to think the change might be in myself, I fretted over it in secret.

M. Jacques, who had now left us and taken a little lodging close at hand, was working hard at his designs; but he came every afternoon for an hour or more to talk French with Louis, and it was Edith's greatest pleasure to be present at these times. One day as she sat apart, not joining in the conversation, but listening to it intently, I happened to catch the expression of her face, and I was surprised, and, at the same time, I am sorry to say, a little mortified, to see that the sad anxious look, which not all my words of love had been able to chase away, was gone. She looked brighter and happier than I had ever seen her. It was at this moment that M. Jacques, who has a loving and tender regard for her, and who, although he does not often address a remark to her, seems always aware of her presence, turned and caught her glance. He looked pleased, and said in a low voice, so gentle that it sounded soft as a caress, "You are listening then, too, *mon enfant?*"

"I always listen when you speak," answered Edith quietly.

The conversation went on, but I did not hear it; I was thinking of Edith and M. Jacques. When he and Louis had gone, and Edith and I were alone, I told her that I believed she cared more for M. Jacques than for any of us.

To my surprise she did not deny it, "He is my benefactor," she said. "Should I not love him? He saved me. You say he was so poor when you found him—almost starving;" tears filled her eyes—"and yet he gave all that day, and money—much money—just as if he had been a rich man; yes, and asked a favour, too, of people of high rank to put me in a place of safety. It would be strange if I did not love him."

"Yes, yes," I said impatiently, "and I love him too. We have cause to be grateful to him—Mother and I; but you should love old friends better than new. We were your friends before you ever heard of M. Jacques, Edith."

"I know you were my friends," answered Edith. "I am grateful to you for all your goodness."

"Grateful to me!" I cried, the tears starting to my eyes. "What do you mean, Edith?"

"My dear Marie," said my friend, "it is foolish of you to distress yourself like this. Do you not see that there are some things which cannot be altered? I am of the people. I was born so, and M. Jacques is of the people. We belong to one another, but you are of a Noble family."

"What does that matter?" I cried. I would have told her what my father always says when this subject is talked of before him, how there can be no greater distinction than that of a noble heart; but she shook her head and refused to listen to me further.

Alas! I began to see what shadow had come between us. Edith had learned since we parted to resent the pride of race, which, as my father says, has ruined our old French nobility. She was proud too. I understood her feeling; but I did think it hard that she should include us among the aristocrats.

After this conversation several weeks passed quietly away. The heat in London was very great, and we all began to pine for country air; but the physicians still urged my mother to keep Louis a little longer under their care.

One afternoon when Louis was unable to come down as usual, and Edith was spending the day with us, Father brought M. Jacques into the parlour, where we were sitting over our sewing-work.

They entered into conversation; and Edith and I, being deeply interested, sat silent listening. M. Jacques, as it seemed, had received some exciting news from France that day. A great wrong had been done, and the thought of it moved him. As he spoke, with a rapidity and vehemence which made it hard to follow him, he started up from his seat, looking for a moment so like the M. Jacques of old that I confess I was frightened. I glanced at Edith, wondering how his excitement would affect her. To my astonishment I saw that over her also a change had come. She sat listening, her head a little thrown back, her hands clenched, her eyes fixed on M. Jacques. But I saw more; and if I was surprised at first, I was soon filled with the deepest wonder, for M. Jacques' expression—I can describe it best as a mingling of pain, defiance, and hopelessness—was repeated on Edith's face. Like a flash of lightning the haunting resemblance that had escaped me so often fixed itself. At that moment Edith and M. Jacques were like enough to have been father and daughter!

I looked at my father, and saw to my surprise that he was watching them too. Had he seen what I had seen? I had not time to settle the question, for, noticing our agitation, he changed the subject of conversation; and M. Jacques, being distressed that he should have been betrayed into showing so much excitement before us, resisting all our entreaties that he would remain and drink tea with us, soon went away.

I was restless and excited that evening. I longed to speak to my father, but he gave me no opportunity. The next morning, however, when breakfast was over, he called me to him.

"Marie," he said, "did you not once tell me that Edith has a locket which was given to her by her nurse?"

"Yes, Father," I answered; "and she has it still. But why—why do you ask?"

"Because, my child, I think the time has come when I may tell you of the suspicion that has been growing upon me."

At this my heart beat high. "If you have seen it—" I began.

"My little Marie," said my father gently, "I cannot allow you to excite yourself. That you and I have seen, or fancy we have seen, a likeness between Edith and M. Jacques, does not make it certain that they are anything to one another. There are many such coincidences in life. And think how cruel it would be to both of them to raise hopes in their minds that might never be fulfilled. It is the truth we want, not romance; and if you are to help me to find out the truth you must be wise and self-controlled."

"I will—I will. See, Father! I am quite calm now. It was only the surprise. Tell me exactly what to do, and I will obey you."

"That is right," said my dear father approvingly. "I knew I could trust you. The first step must be to get hold of Edith's locket. Do you think she would let you have it?"

"I think she might. She does not like to part with it; but if I made her doing so a personal favour—I might say that I had described the locket to you, and that you would like to see the design."

"Yes, that would do. Then we must let it fall into M. Jacques' hands as though by accident. If he recognizes it, this will be a strong point in proof of our suspicion."

"Surely it would be everything."

"No, not quite; for who knows how the nurse got hold of it? However, I think that could soon be explained."

"Yes, yes. Oh, Father, how I wish tomorrow would come! I long to set to work."

"But remember, you promised me to be patient," said my father warningly.

It had been arranged before that Edith was to dine with us on the following day. She arrived at the usual time, and looked the same as ever. What I had expected I do not exactly know, but to see her so quiet and unaltered gave me quite a shock in my excitement. After dinner, when she and I were alone in the parlour, I asked her to be kind enough to show me her locket. I thought she seemed surprised, but she at once did as I wished; and when, my voice trembling a little, I asked her to leave it for two or three days in my keeping, as I wanted my father to see the design, she unfastened it from the ribbon round her neck and put it in my hand. "I would not trust it to everybody," she said; "it has been so long my only treasure that sometimes it seems like a living thing to me. But I know you will take care of it."

"Indeed—indeed I will," I answered. I felt almost like a traitor to my friend for not telling her more; but, remembering Father's warning and my own promise, I managed to keep quiet.

Edith, who I am sure saw and felt the strangeness of my manner, for I could not conceal my restlessness, seemed a little sad all that day, and she left us much earlier than usual.

"Come again very soon, dear Edith," said Louis as she kissed him and said goodbye. "Why, Marie, look here!" he called out, "Edith is crying! What is the matter?"

"It is nothing—nothing," said Edith, trying to get away, for he held her hand. "Goodbye, goodbye, dear Louis!"

"But when will you come again?" he persisted.

"I don't know—perhaps never," she cried; then, seeing she had wounded Louis, she added gently, "I will come again when Marie wants me."

"That will be very soon," I answered gaily. In spite of Louis' distress and Edith's sadness I could not be miserable; I felt so sure that we were going to discover something good.

The next day was the great day on which so much depended. We had, of course, taken Mother into our confidence; and early in the afternoon, when M. Jacques was expected, she and I and Father went into the parlour to wait for him. Mother and I were working, or trying to work; the locket, at which I could not help continually glancing, lay on the table between us; Father, whom I had never seen so excited, was walking up and down silently, and now and then looking at his watch. At last the door opened, and after a few moments' delay M. Jacques, appearing unusually tired and worn, was shown in.

Mother rose to greet him with even more than her ordinary kindliness. After saying that she did not think Louis could see him yet, she made him sit down close beside her. It was long since she had talked with him, she said. She had many questions to ask him. For nearly half an hour dear Mother bore the whole burden of the conversation, for Father and I were worse than useless. M. Jacques was silent at first, but she drew him on to speak of his art, and by degrees he grew eloquent on the subject. At last the critical moment came. There had been a brief silence; and then Mother, whose hand trembled ever so little, took up the locket.

"Talking of designs, M. Jacques," she said, "there is a curious piece of workmanship here that fell into my hands rather strangely the other day. It is quaint and took my fancy. Is it of any value?"

As she spoke she gave him the locket, and, little dreaming of all that might hang upon his next words, M. Jacques walked slowly with it to the window. For a moment there was silence in the room so intense that one might have heard a pin drop, and then there came to our ears a low cry like that of some creature in pain. In the next instant M. Jacques had flown to my mother and was kneeling down before her.

"For God's sake, madam," he gasped, "tell me where—where—?" and here his voice became choked, he buried his face in his hands, and awful sobs shook his whole frame.

I can scarcely write of it. It was terrible— terrible—to see a man so moved. Unable to

bear the sight of his agony I rushed out of the
room, only to find that the marvels of this mar-
vellous day were not over.

In my excitement I had not heard the outside
sounds, but I found that the door had been opened,
and in the hall stood Edith herself, looking white,
poor darling! and a little scared. It was no wonder; as she told me later my face was enough to
frighten anyone. While I gazed at her in a bewildered way—she had come so opportunely that
I doubted whether she was really herself or only
a vision—she seized my arm.

"What is it?" she cried; "speak, Marie, for
pity's sake; Louis—?"

"Louis is better—all right," I said. "Oh! I don't
know what to say; it is of you that I am thinking. How is it that you are here?"

"How is it?" echoed Edith, who thought, I
believe, that I had taken leave of my senses.
"I came because I was cross yesterday, and I
wanted you to forgive me. Madame de Ville
and the children are at the house of a lady close
by. I have only five minutes to spare. Marie,
what is it? Why do you look at me so?"

"Edith," I said, taking both her hands in mine,
"something has happened. No, do not look
so sorrowful; it is good, better than you can
imagine; come with me." I took her hand, and
we went together to the parlour. Edith was as
pale as death. "Courage!" I whispered as I threw
the door open. I was the first to go in, for Edith
had hung back, and for a moment I paused,
feeling not frightened but bewildered. M. Jacques,
from whose eyes the light of reason seemed

to have fled, stood in the centre of the room, waving his arms about, and talking wildly; my father was trying to soothe him; my mother stood apart, with clasped hands and eyes uplifted to heaven. She was praying for peace to descend on this troubled heart.

At the sound of the door as it opened Father turned, and, seeing me, motioned that I should withdraw; but for the first time in my life I ventured to disobey him. A power not my own seemed to be urging me on.

Still leading Edith, I went straight to where M. Jacques stood, and taking his hand placed it in hers. He looked at her and then at me. There was a strange dazed expression on his face, as if he were asleep and trying to awake. Then gradually the perplexity seemed to pass away, and it appeared almost as if a veil were falling from his eyes.

"Antoinette! my Antoinette!" he murmured. Moved by one impulse we fell upon our knees. "M. Jacques," I said, "your Antoinette cannot come back to you; but I have brought you your child Louise Edith—whom you have lost so long. God has taken care of her for you."

What followed I do not exactly know, for my self-control forsook me, and I fell to weeping violently. When I came to myself I was lying on the sofa in Mother's room, and she was beside me. She told me that M. Jacques was quite calm, and that he had no doubt Edith was his long-lost child. He had recognized the locket at once, for it was his own workmanship.

As soon as Father had considered it safe, she

went on to say, he had left the two alone together.
What passed between them then we do not know,
nor do we even desire to hear. When, after many
hours, Mother went softly to them, she found
them sitting hand in hand in the fast deepening
twilight.

That night, when we were gathered together
for evening prayer, Father thanked God in a few
solemn words for the great happiness that had
been vouchsafed to us. It was a moment of
intense feeling—even the servants could not re-
strain their tears. I wonder if M. Jacques'
mother looked down from heaven upon us, and
knew that after many days her words had come
true, for it was through the locket and the gold
pieces that her son had found his child.

August 15th—It is extraordinary how quickly
M. Jacques and Edith have fallen into their new
relation to one another. After the day of which
I have written Edith returned no more to Madame
de Ville. She remained with us until M. Jacques
could receive her, which he very quickly arranged to do. We had quite a little festival on
the day Edith went home, as she called the tiny
lodging where she and her father were to live
for a time. All of us, including Louis, escorted
her thither, and remained to drink tea. Edith did
the honours shyly, but with the natural grace
that belongs to her nation. Her face, which was
beaming with a soft happiness, seemed to have
something new in it; and for the first time since
I had met her she reminded me of Toinette. I
ventured to say this to M. Jacques, but he shook
his head. "I thought so once," he said; "but no

she is like her mother—her mother—" There were tears in his eyes as he turned away.

It would be difficult to imagine two people more utterly and thoroughly contented with one another than were these two in the first days of their reunion. The isolation that had been so galling to their warm natures was over; each had found someone to live for, and in the sunshine of happiness all the underlying bitterness in their hearts had melted away. I must not linger over all the good things that this delightful discovery has brought about, for I have one more incident to relate.

My father, feeling that the recognition of Edith as M. Jacques' daughter ought not to rest entirely on her possession of a locket that had formerly belonged to her father, and a fancied resemblance to him, determined to set on foot inquiries about Mrs. Sinclair, who would, of course, be able to explain how Edith came into her keeping.

Lest we should be frightened or excited, Father kept his own counsel, and I only heard the other day what he had done. It appears that he had much trouble in tracing Mrs. Sinclair. Hearing, however, after many inquiries, that she was living in a village called Hampstead near London, in a very humble way, he set out thither one day, accompanied by M. Jacques. They found the cottage to which they were directed, and M. Jacques stayed outside, while my father knocked at the door, and asked for Mrs. Sinclair. Some little difficulty was made about admitting him; but Father, when he chooses, has an authoritative way with him, and upon his telling the little servant girl that he had come to see her mistress, she fell back and allowed him to do as he pleased.

Mrs. Sinclair was in the little parlour, and in her usual state of morning *déshabille*. She screamed out when she saw my father, and being, I suppose, too really frightened even to pretend to faint, demanded angrily what he wanted. He said that he had come to ask her some questions, which it would be well for her own sake that she should answer truthfully. Upon this she commenced a violent attack upon Edith, whose conduct, she said, had brought her to misery.

Father waited till this outburst was over, and then said that unless she told him all she knew of Edith's history, he would put the matter into the hands of others who might not deal so gently with her. For a long time she protested that she knew nothing, until at length my father told her that further deception was useless. Edith's father, he proceeded to say, had been found and was outside. If she could not make up her mind at once to relate what she knew, she would have to reckon with him. Mrs. Sinclair had doubtless heard of Edith's father as a fierce and violent man, who shrank from nothing to serve his own purposes, for this last threat completely vanquished her. After making my father promise to protect her from his vengeance, she told her story.

The daughter of a Creole, who was the manager of large estates in the West Indies belonging to the Marquis de la Fontenaye, she had married an Englishman, had come over to Europe, and had lived for a time in Paris, where she and her husband were often made use of by the Marquis. Later on they settled in England; but the marquis did not lose sight of them, and when he was casting about him for some person to whose care he might entrust his grandchild, his thoughts reverted to Mrs. Sinclair. She was then a widow, and the very considerable addition to her income promised by the Marquis was no small boon to her.

The money for Edith was paid liberally and regularly until the Revolution began, since which time no word from the Marquis had ever reached her, nor did she know whether he was alive or dead.

Such was the story which my father heard. He wrote it down at Mrs. Sinclair's dictation, and forced her to sign her name to it. Then, having promised that she should be no further disturbed, he hastened to rejoin M. Jacques, who was waiting in an agony of impatience, and to assure him that there was now no room for doubt—Edith was indeed his child.

For my part I hope that we shall never hear Mrs. Sinclair's name again. Father says she complained bitterly of Tom's wild courses—I only trust that he, too, may never more cross our path.

I think I shall write no further in this house, for Mother has made up her mind that Louis will be better in the country, and we are to return home almost immediately. The very thought of seeing our dear home again fills me with joy, and Louis looks brighter than he has done for some weeks; so after all it will be with happy, hopeful hearts that we shall set out on our homeward journey. Even the parting from Edith will lose half its bitterness by the knowledge that she is with her father; and M. Jacques has promised to bring her to see us before long.

CHAPTER XVIII

HOME AGAIN

SEPTEMBER 1st—Our dear old home again! How calm and unaltered everything appears! How refreshing to our eyes, weary of the great city with its never-ceasing rush and hurry and din, are the sights and sounds of the country! The garden is gorgeous with autumn flowers; the trees are just touched with the faintest tinge of yellow, and the birds are beginning to gather on the church-tower to consult about their winter flight. We have missed the full glory of summer, but the sweet quiet of autumn time is yet to come.

September 3rd—Louis is better. What happiness it gives me to write these three simple words! Better! Then perhaps he will be well again soon—able to talk and laugh and ride and dance, as he used to do in the days before we went to London. He is indeed quiet still, and he does not seem in his old spirits; but he eats with appetite, and his eyes are brighter than they have been of late, and the faintest colour has

come into his cheeks. Oh, Louis, my darling!
my brother! I do not think that, until today, I
ever knew how much I loved you.

September 6th—We are a little disappointed
about Louis; he is certainly better, but he is not
so cheerful as we should like to see him, nor does
he seem to care to shake off his invalid ways.
Our doctor says he wants rousing, and I have
been doing my best to amuse him, with, I am
sorry to say, no very great success. Can it be
that my society is not enough for him now—that
he misses all the coming and going of our London
life? This thought gave me so great a pang that
I could not help speaking of it to my father today. I hoped, no doubt, that he would contradict
me. We were walking through the village together when I began to speak of Louis. Father
listened as usual with the greatest attention to
all I had to say. He did not, however, console
me after the fashion I had expected, for, so far
from contradicting me, he seemed to be of the
same mind. "I think it not at all unlikely," he
said, "that Louis misses some of the friends he
used to see in London."

I suppose the colour mounted to my face at
these words, for he looked at me smilingly, and
drew my hand within his arm.

"My little Marie," he said, "must learn the
lesson her father tried to learn many years ago.
We may love as deeply as we please, but we
must not make a prisoner of our love. Do you
understand what I mean, my child?"

"Yes, Father, I think I do."

"There is all the difference in the world between loving for our own sakes and loving for the sake of those we love. The first kind is of earth, the second of heaven. But you can't understand all this yet. Let us come back to Louis. What if we brought some of his friends to him?"

As he asked this question we came within sight of the old house in the village, where Mrs. Sinclair used to live. To my surprise I saw that the doors and windows were open, and that workmen were busy within. "Oh dear!" I cried out. "Then someone has taken the old house again. I am so sorry."

"Yes," said my father, looking at me with a peculiar smile. "Someone has taken it; but why should you be sorry, Marie? You found one romance in the old house—you might possibly find another."

"Father!" I cried, "I believe you are doing this!"

"Doing what, Marie?"

"You said you would bring Louis' friends to him. Do you mean—?"

"I mean this house for your friend Edith and her father, my little Marie, and as you know more about their tastes than I do, probably you will give me some advice about fitting it up and furnishing it."

I could not speak, but I think my eyes must have spoken for me, for Father did not seem disappointed at the way in which I took his news. As soon as I had recovered from my first astonishment we went over the house and discussed various alterations and improvements. It seems

like a dream—like a story out of a fairy-book—
that Edith should come back to the house where
she was so miserable and live there in peace with
her father.

I hastened home with my news. Mother, of
course, had heard it before, but to Louis it was as
great a surprise as it had been to me, and we spent
a most delightful hour in planning what we could
do to give pleasure to Edith and M. Jacques.
Father came in while we were talking, and I could
see by the expression of his face that he was pleased
with Louis' animation, which, indeed, is one of
the best and most hopeful of signs. Before we parted
for the night he gave us a sum of money, which
we might spend, he said, on the decoration of the
house. For the next few days we shall have plenty
to do in considering how we can lay out our money
profitably.

September 10th—There is already the greatest
change in Louis. Instead of having his breakfast brought to him in bed, he is up and out early
in the morning looking after the workmen, who
are still busy in the old house. Then, when he
comes home, there is no time for the midday rest,
which had become a habit with him. In spite of
Mother's fears that he is doing too much he must
have long consultations with the housekeeper or
with me, and in the afternoon we must drive or
ride to the towns and villages in the neighbourhood to hunt for pretty furniture and china and
pictures for the dear old house. The garden and
the little greenhouse have to be looked after also,
for everything had fallen into disrepair, and Louis
and I are determined to have all in order before

Edith and M. Jacques arrive. I hear, by the by, that M. Jacques' designs, which Father had presented to the notice of some well-known manufacturers, have become famous, and that he can now earn more than enough to keep himself and his daughter in comfort. This is a piece of news which delights us all.

September 30th—How slowly the last few days passed by! I thought they would never come to an end. But they are over now, and Edith is amongst us, and Louis is growing stronger and brighter every day, and all the trouble of the past year seems like an unhappy dream.

Yesterday was the great day. We had arranged everything beforehand. My father and I were to drive to the nearest town to meet Edith and M. Jacques, who were to come from London by the mail-coach. Mother and Louis were to give the last finishing touches to the house, and to be in the porch to meet our friends, so that they might feel they were indeed coming home.

I must confess I was glad to have been the one chosen to go to the town, for I am afraid if I had remained at the house I should never have been able to keep patient.

It was a glorious day. The bright sunshine made the yellow leaves on the trees gleam like gold, the sky was blue, and the tenderest gray mist hung over the distant hills.

We arrived at the post-town about noon, and instead of going to the inn where we usually put up, turned, by Father's orders, down a small street, which was almost blocked by our chariot. Before a little inn in this street we drew up. I had been somewhat puzzled when Father passed by the place where we usually stop when we go to the town; but no sooner had I looked in the face of the woman who came out to greet us than I understood why he had decided to put up at her house. This was Edith's friend, the kind, good woman who had taken her in on the morning after her flight.

I glanced at my father, who gave me a smile of assent. How like him to have found out this, I thought! He, in the meanwhile, was speaking to the woman in his gentlest and most courteous fashion. He said we should be glad to rest at her house for an hour, and was her husband at home, as he wished to see him. She led us in, not without many an apology for the lowliness of her dwelling, and, having begged us to be seated, went off in search of her goodman. In a few moments they returned together, and then Father asked if they had not sheltered a young girl who was escaping from her friends during the terrible snowstorm of January last. At this the woman looked alarmed, but the man answered boldly:

"Aye, your honour, and many's the sleepless night I have passed thinking of the poor lass! My mind misgave me about letting her go, but she was a gentle lass, and she begged us hard not to stop her—"

"John," interrupted the woman stoutly, "she was a good lass, and told the truth, that I know; and if so be as she came to me again I would take her in, and thou woudst not be the one to say me nay."

"My good people," said my father, rising and

holding out his hand, "you did nobly. But for you this young girl might have perished in the snow. I have come to tell you that every word she spoke was true. But her troubles are over now. She has found her father, and we expect her to arrive with him by the coach this very afternoon. My daughter and I would like you to come with us to meet her. You were the only ones to bid her Godspeed when she set out on her terrible journey, and it is just that you should be amongst the first to welcome her."

To describe the astonishment and delight of the good couple at this news would be impossible. They soon, however, recovered from their first embarrassment, and listened attentively while we told them of Edith's adventures in London, and how strangely and happily we had discovered her.

The hour for the arrival of the coach was close at hand, and the mistress of the house bustled about to prepare dinner for the travelers and for us. When all was ready she put on her bonnet and went out with us to the High Street to watch for the first sight of the coach.

We stood in a little group, my father and these good people and I, and to me it seemed as if minutes had never passed so slowly. "Is it time? is it time?" I kept asking, and my father would answer, "Two minutes more—one minute. Be patient, Marie. The horses cannot travel as quickly as your thoughts."

At last we heard the sound of horses trotting, and the coach rattling noisily over the stony street. Nearer they came and nearer. I gave a

cry. "There they are! There they are! I see
M. Jacques' head, and Edith! Edith! Oh! Father,
how slowly they come!"

"Nay, mistress, the pace be fast enough," said
our friend of the inn; and while he was speaking
the great lumbering carriage drew up, the door
was thrown open, M. Jacques stepped out, gave
his hand to Edith, and led her towards us.
Which of us kissed her first, or what was said,
or how she cried when she saw her kind friends
of the inn, or after what fashion Father persuaded
us not to block up the main road, but to carry
ourselves and our happiness to the quiet little
house where our dinner was waiting, I am afraid
I cannot say. I was too much excited to remember anything distinctly.

Over the dinner-table, at which we insisted
that the master and mistress of the inn should
take their place, we became more composed, and
then there was so much to be said that Father
was forced to remind us of the long drive we had
before us, and of the impatience of those at home.

"Ah! poor Louis," I cried. "I had forgotten
him. Father, we must start at once."

"You will bring our lass to see us again," said
the kind mistress of the inn to M. Jacques.

"Madame," he replied feelingly, "in this and
in everything else you may command my services.
They are worth very little, it is true, but such as
they are they are yours. It had been our inten-
tion to seek you out and entreat you to accept
our gratitude and friendship. Mr. Hamilton, my
friend and benefactor, has, as is usual with him,
gone before our wishes." So far he spoke fluently,

but now his voice shook. "I would say much more," he faltered, "I cannot. God has been gracious to me. I distrusted Him once. I said everything was against me. He has been better to me than I deserved."

"Not better, Father," whispered Edith, whose eyes were full of tears. I was weeping too, and our host and hostess looked sorrowful as we bade them goodbye. Indeed it was a day of rain and sunshine, but the rain was like summer showers, and the sunshine was always to be seen behind the clouds. When we came to the old house, and saw dearest Mother standing with smiles of welcome in the pretty porch, and Louis looking like a young prince in the ruby velvet suit which he had put on—vain boy—in honour of the occasion, a few steps in advance of her; when we led M. Jacques in, and took him to the workroom which we had prepared for him; when we showed Edith her parlour, and her withdrawing-room, and the little glass house for flowers, all of which were to be her very own; when we sat down all together and talked of the past and of the future; and when Louis, and Edith, and I, falling off from the conversation of the elder people, had one of our long delightful talks, which—and that is the best of it—is only the first of many, we felt as if we could never be miserable again.

They are calling me, and I must put my diary aside. I thought they would have been perfectly happy—my own dear Louis and Edith—but it seems that they cannot do without me. I wonder if it is wrong to feel glad that it should be so.

December 31st—Three months since I have

written a line in my book! Can it be? My book, to which I poured out all my troubles in the dark and dreadful days of the early part of this year. How faithless of me to have forgotten it!

And yet, as I look back, it seems to me that there has not been much to put down. We have been happy; but that is so quickly said, and no doubt the happiest times are those about which there is nothing much to tell.

To make the story of this year complete, and to remind myself of the many reasons I have for deep thankfulness on this the last hour of its last day, I will briefly trace the history of these three months. We soon grew accustomed to having Edith and M. Jacques for neighbours. We met every day, for Louis continued to take lessons in French from him, and Edith and I pursued many of our studies together. As Louis continues delicate—the doctors say that he will never be so strong as others—Father has decided that he shall not leave home for any school or college; and since he must be educated, a tutor has been engaged to teach him Greek, Latin, and mathematics. From Father he learns to ride and to fence, and from M. Jacques drawing as well as French. In the early hours of the day we are both busy with our studies; but as Mother will not allow Louis to work after dinner, which we take at one o'clock, we have all the afternoon for amusement, and no amusement is ever considered complete by either of us without Edith. We play tennis sometimes in the court above the picture-gallery, and sometimes we take long rides across the country, and there are old people in the village whom we visit together, taking them little comforts to help them through the long dark winter days. It is a pleasure also to watch M. Jacques at his work, and to listen to the tales of which he has an inexhaustible store.

Both Edith and he have changed. He is much gentler than he used to be, indeed it is touching to see how he considers others, and how careless he would be of his own comfort if his daughter did not look after him. And Edith, what shall I say of her? I loved her from the first, as my book knows, but then she often troubled me, and there was sorrow as well as pleasure in my affecttion. Now the sorrow has gone, and only the pleasure remains. Happiness has made her what God intended she should be—bright, high-spirited, and joyous. My prayer for her on this last day of the year is that her happiness may go on and increase. But if trouble comes, as I suppose it must come some day to her and to us all, I am sure she will be much better able to meet it for these happy days. My father says that happiness once given is an eternal possession. It may seem to go away, but it lives on in memory, and nothing but our own deed can separate us from it.

That is a good thought for this New Year's Eve. The sorrow of this wonderful year has gone by, the happiness remains. It is ours forever, the gift of our Father in heaven, which no one can take away from us. I thank Him for it, and I go on with hope and gladness, trusting that He will help me to be good, and humble, and unselfish in the year that is opening now.

CHAPTER XIX

CONCLUSION

WITH a deep sigh Marie Hamilton closed the book containing the story of the joys and sorrows of those so long passed away, yet her own kindred.

She threw herself down on the grass, looked up at the yew-trees, and was just about to fall to dreaming, when a gentle hand was laid on her shoulder.

"Come, Marie," said Mrs. Hamilton, "I can't give you any more time to yourself. Lunch is ready, and you ought to be starving."

"Oh, Mother!" cried Marie, "who could think of being hungry on a broiling day like this, and with such a book in one's hand?"

"It interested you, then?" said Mrs. Hamilton.

"Interested me!" returned Marie, "I shall not be able to think of anything else for days. Now, dear Mother, do sit down by me for a few minutes and let us talk about it. I have a puzzle that I want you to explain. Marie Hamilton was my great-grandmother?" you to explain. Marie Hamilton was my great-grandmother?"

"Yes, Marie."

"But how can that be? When she married she must have had another name. It was Louis who ought to have been our ancestor."

"Quite right, Marie, he ought to have been."

"Oh, don't say that he died after all!" cried Marie.

Mrs. Hamilton smiled. "He died like the rest of them, Marie," she answered. "Why, he would have been a hundred years old if he had lived until now. But he did not die early, in fact he lived for many years after his marriage."

"He married Edith, of course?"

"Yes, he married Edith."

"Then why—?"

"Wait a moment, you impatient child. Louis and Edith, I was going to tell you, had no children. Marie, who married a Frenchman of Noble birth, had two sons and several daughters. Her second son was adopted by his uncle, Louis Hamilton, took his name, and inherited the estates. That second son, who was born early in the century, was your father's father."

"Oh, how interesting!" cried Marie. "And—"

"My dear child, we must not stop now. Lunch is waiting, and you know you have to prepare for your friends who are coming this afternoon. Someday I may perhaps hunt up some more family records for you. In the meantime, my Marie, I want you to lay to heart what you have

read in this book. Walk always, as the Marie of
its story did, in the path of unselfish duty, and
your history, though it may be only that of an
everyday life, will be lovingly remembered by
those who come after you."

THE END

Historical Fiction by William W. Canfield

THE WHITE SENECA
Illustrated by G. A. Harker

In the year 1774, fifteen-year-old Henry Cochrane is captured by a party of Seneca Indians near his home in central New York State. Adopted by the young Seneca, Hiokoto the Hawk, Henry grows to love the Indian ways and becomes Dundiswa — the White Seneca. When Henry is captured by an enemy tribe, he must rely on all the skills he has learned from the Indians, as well as his own courage and determination, as he attempts to escape from them and rescue fellow captive, Constance Leonard.

Meanwhile, the Revolutionary War has begun and conflict escalates between the Indians, who have sided with the British, and the settlers. Eventually Henry must choose between his love for the Senecas and his loyalty to his own people.

AT SENECA CASTLE
Illustrated by G. A. Harker

In this sequel to *The White Seneca*, Henry Cochrane, now eighteen, is entrusted with a message from the settlers of the Wyoming Valley, Pennsylvania, to the Continental Army. They are suffering under the constant Indian raids instigated by the British and plead for protection. Because of Henry's knowledge of Indian ways, General George Washington requests his services as a scout for General Sullivan in the campaign to forever break the power of the Iroquois Confederacy. In the fall of 1779, the combined armies of Generals Sullivan and Clinton sweep across New York State, destroying Indian villages and crops. Henry, alone and in constant peril, travels ahead of the Army seeking to warn his Indian friends of the coming destruction while also desperately searching for the beautiful Constance Leonard whom he had been forced to leave in captivity a year earlier.

WWW.SALEMRIDGEPRESS.COM

More Historical Fiction

THE SIGN ABOVE THE DOOR
by William W. Canfield

Eight plagues have come upon the land of Egypt and the nation is gripped with fear. The Egyptian nobles watch in dismay as their aging Pharaoh stubbornly refuses to listen to the demands of the Hebrew God. Young Prince Martiesen is adon of the most prosperous region in Lower Egypt, which includes the land of Goshen where the Hebrews live. He has been forced by Pharaoh to further increase the burden of the Hebrews yet Martiesen himself is in love with the beautiful Hebrew maiden, Elisheba, whom he is forbidden by Egyptian law to marry. In his own household, unbeknownst to Martiesen, his new scribe, Peshala, is plotting evil against him. As the nation despairs, the nobles turn to Martiesen for leadership, but before he can decide what to do, Elisheba is kidnapped by Peshala and terrifying darkness falls over the land.

GYTHA'S MESSAGE
A Tale of Saxon England
by Emma Leslie
Illustrated by C. J. Staniland R. I.

Saxon England in 1053 is a time of violence, cruelty and ignorance where the strong dominate and mercy and compassion are scarce. Young Gytha longs to leave behind the evil of the world and enter a convent where she can devote herself to learning more about the God who loves even a little slave girl. Instead she lives in a household that scorns the very name of Christ. Gytha's mistress, the Lady Hilda, is an invalid whose afflictions have made her fretful and cross, yet as Gytha lives out her simple faith in service to her mistress, she is able to bring hope and purpose to Hilda's life. When England is defeated in 1066 by William the Conqueror, Gytha and Hilda face their greatest challenge—trusting God when it seems as though He has turned His back on England. Through all of her trials, Gytha learns that God often has a greater work for us to do *in* the world than *out* of it.

WWW.SALEMRIDGEPRESS.COM